RACHEL'S COMING HOME

When her parents run into difficulties running their boarding kennels, Rachel Collington decides to resign from her job and return home to help out. The first customer she encounters is arrogant Philip Milligan, who is nowhere near as friendly as his two collies. Gradually though, he begins to thaw — but just as Rachel is wondering if she has misjudged him, it seems that someone is intent on sabotaging the kennels' reputation.

GILLIAN VILLIERS

RACHEL'S COMING HOME

Complete and Unabridged

LINFORD
Leicester

First published in Great Britain in 2009

First Linford Edition
published 2010

British Library CIP Data

Villiers, Gillian.
  Rachel's coming home.- -
(Linford romance library)
1. Pet boarding facilities- -Fiction.
2. Dog owners- -Fiction. 3. Sabotage- -
Fiction. 4. Love stories. 5. Large type books.
I. Title II. Series
823.9′2–dc22

ISBN 978–1–44480–150–7

Published by
F. A. Thorpe (Publishing)
Anstey, Leicestershire

Set by Words & Graphics Ltd.
Anstey, Leicestershire
Printed and bound in Great Britain by
T. J. International Ltd., Padstow, Cornwall

This book is printed on acid-free paper

A Change Of Pace

Everyone seemed to think Rachel Collington was the sort of person who couldn't cope when things got difficult. Maybe it was because she was small and slight with a pale complexion and soft blonde hair. But they were wrong. Rachel knew she could cope with anything, if she had to. The only problem was persuading other people, and in particular her mother, of this.

'Of course I'm going to come home. I'm going to come and look after you both. How could you think otherwise?' Rachel spoke firmly into the telephone receiver, willing her mother to be convinced. She hated arguing with her mother.

'But Rachel, darling, you have such a good job. You can't give that up. Your father and I are so pleased at how you've settled in Liverpool, even if it is

1

a little further away than we would have liked.'

'The job has been fine, Mum. But now I'm coming home.' Rachel smiled to herself as she said the words. She had been mulling over this idea for a while. Events had just speeded up her decision.

'Really, it's not necessary. Your father and I have decided. We'll just have to put off any clients booked for the next month and then we'll see how things go. We don't like to do it, of course, especially at the moment.' Her mother's voice wavered then she collected herself and said firmly, 'I'm hopeful people will understand.'

'You can't cancel bookings,' said Rachel quickly. 'People will already have arranged their holidays, happy in the knowledge that you and Dad will be looking after their darling dogs. It would be awful to cancel at this late stage.'

'I know that, dear.' Rachel's mother sighed. She sounded tired. Rachel wished she could go home right now, but there were still two days until the end of term.

When her father had taken early retirement five years ago, her parents had opened Collington Boarding Kennels in the Southern Uplands of Scotland. It had been a dream come true. Unfortunately, her mother had been diagnosed with rheumatoid arthritis two years later and was finding the work increasingly difficult. Her father falling on a newly-sluiced kennel floor and breaking his ankle badly had been the incident which precipitated Rachel's decision.

'Don't cancel any bookings yet,' said Rachel firmly. 'I'll be home on Saturday. And Anthony's there, isn't he? You said you weren't very busy this week, surely he can help out.' She tried to sound more certain than she felt. Anthony, her younger brother, was on a 'gap' year. This was supposed to involve a mixture of working and travelling but as far as Rachel could tell there hadn't been much of either so far.

'He has been very good about driving me to and from the hospital,' said her mother cautiously. Rachel could imagine why. Anthony's main love in life, apart from his bed, was cars.

'That's good,' she said. 'Get him to walk the dogs for you. Mum, please don't try to do it yourself. Just think what would happen if you were to have a fall as well.'

'I'm being very careful,' said her mother so hastily that Rachel knew she was doing too much. 'My knees have been much better recently. It's wonderful what these new drugs can do.'

Rachel was delighted that her mother was being prescribed the new, more expensive drugs for her arthritis, and that they were being so successful. She just worried this would make her mother push herself too hard. She wondered if she should try and speak to Anthony, to make sure he was pulling his weight. Then she decided she would be better off waiting until the weekend when they could speak face to face.

'It's wonderful you're feeling better, but I really don't think you should do too much. Please, Mum? You need to save your strength for looking after Dad when he gets home.'

To her relief, her mother could see the sense of this, and they talked for a little longer about likely discharge dates and how good the doctors were being. Eventually, Rachel brought the conversation to an end. She loved chatting to her mother and knew her mother needed her more than ever now. Unfortunately there were other things she had to do.

'Remember,' she said. 'I'll be up as early as I can on Saturday. Definitely before lunch. Don't turn anyone away. Have you any bookings that start before then?'

'Just one, arriving on Saturday morning. A Mr Milligan. He's a new client and he sounded very picky. I don't know about this, Rachel. It might be better just to let him down now. He has two collies and there is no way I'll be able to manage those.'

'Then make sure Anthony is with you until I arrive. Tell him you'll pay him, I'm sure that will help.'

'Yes, dear,' said her mother, sounding doubtful. 'It will be nice to see you . . . '

'It'll be lovely. And it won't just be a visit, this time. I'm coming home for good. Now, I must go. Remember to look after yourself and give my love to Dad.'

Rachel replaced the receiver and as she did so the smile faded from her face. She was more worried about her father than she cared to admit. On top of that, she now had to compose a resignation letter to hand in the next morning, and she knew her headmistress wouldn't be pleased to receive it. She would try to persuade Rachel to stay and Rachel would feel she was letting her down, knowing how much she had learnt from Mrs Dobson. This was what had delayed her decision to resign until now. But she had to be firm. Her family needed her.

⋆　⋆　⋆

Philip Milligan was beginning to think it had been a mistake, returning to Scotland. Everything was so slow here, as though they had barely made it into the twentieth century, never mind the twenty-first. True, that was one of the reasons he had chosen the remote Tweed valley, but now he was having second thoughts.

At first he had been pleased that no one seemed to recognise him. After being mobbed, well, occasionally tailed, in London, it was good to have some peace. Now, however, he was starting to think it would be rather nice if people did know who he was, and gave him the respect and the service he deserved.

He was waiting in a queue at the newsagents. He had been here ten minutes already and there was only one person in front of him. This one person seemed to know the proprietor well, along with almost everyone in the town, and felt the need to check up on the well-being of each and every one of them.

He cleared his throat. 'Excuse me. Perhaps I could just pay for these . . . ?' He indicated the newspaper and journal he held and handed over the correct money.

The solid matron who was serving behind the counter now turned her attention to him. 'Sorry to keep you waiting,' she said, not sounding sorry enough. Then she looked more closely at him. 'Why, aren't you that man off the telly? That history programme? If you just give me a minute I'll remember your name.' She turned to the woman in front of him. 'Do you no' recognise him? I'm sure it's him.'

Philip was flattered and put out in equal measure. It was good to know someone in these backwoods watched his programmes. But now it would be all over town and he would be pestered to talk to goodness knows how many

Women's Rurals and Rotary Clubs and feted as the local celebrity. He really didn't have time for that.

'Aye, I mind you,' said the other woman, sounding disapproving rather than impressed. 'You're the one with the long hair. Did your mother no tell you that a man looks more like a man with a decent short back and sides?'

The observation was so absurd that Philip gave a snort of laughter. These definitely weren't the sort of comments he was used to. He liked the feeling of the dark locks on his shoulders. And hadn't the gossip column of one of the dailies referred to his *Byronic good looks* not so very long ago? He wondered again what kind of place he had come to.

As he left the shop he realised they hadn't even remembered what he was called. So much for being a household name. He shook his head ruefully. The dogs pushed their soft faces into his legs, showing they at least appreciated him. He untied them from the handily placed railing outside the shop — there were some things about country living that he found useful — and set off back up the hill for home.

* * *

Maggie Collington smoothed out the duvet and looked around the little room with pleasure. Rachel had already left home by the time they moved to this house, but the end bedroom was always thought of as 'her' room. Now she would be staying for a good, long time. Maggie loved the idea of having her whole family around her. She hoped they discharged poor John from hospital soon.

She sighed. She was growing anxious about Anthony. He should have been back from Glasgow by now, but he had a habit of running late, so she determined not to worry too much. Rachel said it wasn't good for her and she was sure she was right.

Maggie realised she had taken a little

too long preparing the room. She still had the dogs to feed, something that Anthony would have done if he was home. John didn't like her to carry the heavy buckets but she could manage perfectly well, as long as she took her time. She took a deep breath and carefully descended the stairs, then ventured out into the back yard. The sun was shining and the spring birds singing. Her wrists only twinged a very little when she tipped the buckets.

She paused to watch the tractor in the field to her left. That must be Freddy Smith, ploughing the field in preparation for reseeding. He was certainly a hard working man. A shame he wasn't a little more sociable, but as John said, it took all sorts. Maggie paused to watch the seagulls wheel and dive in the wake of the tractor and then scolded herself for wasting yet more time.

She really wished she wasn't so slow. If she didn't hurry, the morning chores wouldn't be finished by the time Rachel arrived and she was determined her daughter wouldn't spend her first day at home working. She was such a good girl, but she did have this tendency to take over. Maggie liked to think she could manage perfectly well herself, if she stuck at it.

She flushed when she remembered what she had heard the day before in Boroughbie: that the dogs were neglected when John Collington wasn't there. It wasn't true. What a thing to say! Mrs Smart at the butchers had mentioned it to her, saying she thought Maggie should know what people were saying. Maggie gave a little shudder. It definitely wasn't true, but it puzzled her who should be saying these things.

★ ★ ★

Rachel's spirits rose as she turned her little car off the motorway at Moffat and headed up into the hills beyond the town. She had loved this area from the days when family holidays had been spent here, and more so since her parents had moved here permanently. The soft blush of the sun on the rolling green and brown hills and the sparkle of the many streams were such a contrast to her life in Liverpool. Not that there was anything wrong with Liverpool, but she had realised she really wasn't a city person.

It felt good to have finally made the break. Mrs Dobson had been as disappointed by her resignation as Rachel had feared, but her pleas had not changed Rachel's mind. She loved primary school teaching and maybe she would go back to it one day, but it wouldn't be in Liverpool. She was going to make a new life for herself in this wonderful place. Her first task, though, was to help her parents over their current difficulties.

As she drew up before the long, low, white cottage she saw she was not the only arrival. A shiny four-by-four was parked on the gravel drive and a tall man was standing at the front door, apparently waiting for it to be opened.

He looked as though he might have been waiting for a while and Rachel jumped hastily from her car. 'Can I help you?' she said, hurrying forward. 'Rachel Collington,' she said, proffering her hand.

'Are you part of this establishment?' said the man, frowning and giving her hand a cursory shake. 'I've been waiting here a good five minutes. I was told I could arrive any time this morning. It's really not very convenient to have to hang around like this.'

'I'm sorry,' said Rachel. 'I'm sure my mother is about. It's most unlike her not to answer the door at once. But as I'm here now perhaps I can help?'

She squinted up at the man. He was very large and vaguely familiar.

'Perhaps you can.' He was still frowning, seeming unsure as to whether to continue with his complaint. Then the whining of dogs in the back of his smart car decided him. He strode over and opened the door to let them out.

'I've booked Bill and Ben into the kennels here.' He stooped to place a hand on the head of each dog and his expression softened, making him suddenly rather attractive.

Rachel smiled and bent to greet the dogs herself. The two collies were beauties, with thick glossy coats and bright eyes. Maybe, now she was here, she would be able to have a dog of her own. What a wonderful thought.

'My mother said she was expecting you,' said Rachel, glad that she knew this much. 'Why don't you come through and I can show you the set up? Bring any blankets or toys you want to leave with the dogs, it helps if they have something familiar.'

Rachel turned the handle of the front door and was glad to find it open. She was more than a little worried at the non-appearance of her mother.

She led the stranger along the short stone-flagged passageway into the kitchen at the back of the house. From here you could see the courtyard around which the new kennels had been built. To her relief, she spotted her mother coming slowly out of the end building, carrying a bucket in one hand whilst the other held her walking stick.

Forgetting the stranger for a moment she opened the back door and stepped out. 'Mum, what are you doing? You know you shouldn't be carrying anything heavy . . . '

'It's all right, dear,' said her mother, but her voice was breathless. 'It's not heavy.' She put down the bucket which was, in fact, empty. Rachel guessed that it had been rather heavier before her mother began the round of feeding.

She sighed. 'Where's Anthony?'

Her mother frowned meaningfully at her and then turned to smile at the newcomer. 'Mr Milligan? How nice to meet you. Have you just arrived? How fortunate that Rachel was here to let you in.'

'Indeed,' said the man. Rachel was relieved that he didn't launch into a tirade about having been kept standing on the front doorstep. She waited whilst he introduced the two dogs to her mother, who in turn explained how the kennels were run. Her mother still looked a little pale and when she offered to show Mr Milligan around Rachel suggested she took her mother's place. 'Why don't you put the kettle on and sort out the paperwork?' she said brightly. 'I'll enjoy showing Mr Milligan around and seeing what little visitors we have in at the moment.'

The man followed her across the yard, the dogs prancing at his heels. New dogs were always excited by the smells and noise of the kennels and she was secretly impressed that they stayed so close to their master. She found the man rather arrogant but he clearly had a knack with dogs.

As she commenced the brief tour of the kennels, Rachel began to relax. It was a lovely place, still spotless despite her parents' problems, beautifully laid out in a modern design, with every dog having its own small room and a private run. Animals that came from the same family were given a slightly larger *apartment* and Rachel immediately spotted which one was meant for Bill and Ben and indicated this to their owner. She hoped he was impressed.

'I'm sure they'll be very happy here,' she said encouragingly. 'We make sure they get plenty of exercise and are well fed and cared for. In accordance with the owner's instructions, of course.' She patted the head of a little West Highland White terrier as she passed. 'Hello Jinty, how are you sweetheart? We find the dogs are very happy with us and their owners often bring them back again and again.'

'Not quite Holiday Inn standards,' said the man. Rachel wasn't sure if he was being complimentary so she merely smiled. She wished she could remember why the man seemed so familiar. He was good-looking in a rugged kind of way and he certainly had the self assurance that made her think he was someone. Hopefully her mother would be able to explain.

'I'll take you back to the house now,' she said. 'Do you want to keep the dogs with you? They're very welcome in the house. We have different dogs in at different times, so it is quite a home from home for them.'

This was one thing her parents had insisted on when they started the kennels and Rachel knew it was popular with the owners. The man merely nodded and put a hand down to touch each dog again. He hadn't praised the facilities and she felt slighted on her parents' behalf. People were normally quite effusive, as they should be.

The man took his leave soon after, declining the offer of tea. 'I'm in rather a hurry,' he said, glancing at Rachel, but fortunately not mentioning his wait at the door. She felt annoyed with him, but when she saw him kneel to hug each dog in turn she decided to put his abruptness down to parting with the beautiful collies, who he clearly loved.

'He's new to the area, isn't he?' she

said as soon as the four-by-four had drawn away. 'Certainly not one of your normal clients.'

'He seems a very nice man,' said her mother. Rachel smiled. She should have known her mother would say that. She never could see the bad side of anyone.

'As long as he pays, I suppose that's the main thing,' she said. 'Now, tell me how Dad is. And where Anthony is. What a good job I arrived when I did, you look worn out.' Rachel took over the pouring of the tea and collected the biscuit tin from the pantry. She would start the way she intended to continue.

'Your dad is doing very well and looked forward to seeing you later on. As to Anthony. Well, I'm not sure where Anthony is. He didn't come home last night.'

You're The Only Family She Has

Anthony was walking slowly along Buchanan Street, shivering despite the sunshine. He was sure he had had a fleece with him yesterday, but it seemed to have been mislaid. Now his head was pounding and the bright sunshine hurt his eyes and he had no idea how he was going to get home from Glasgow. Missing the final train last night had seemed like a fun thing to do, but now he wasn't so sure.

He pulled his mobile out of the pocket of his jeans and looked at it hopefully. The battery was still completely flat. It might actually have been better if the thief had taken this and left his wallet behind. There hadn't been much money in the wallet after paying for his ticket to the concert, and then a few beers afterwards, but there must have been something.

He fingered the change in his pocket. Eighty-three pence. Either he could try and find a very cheap coffee or he could use it to phone home. He knew his mother would be worrying, she always made a fuss about every little thing, she was sure to panic about his being missing for a whole twelve hours. That thought decided him. He wasn't a child any longer, was he?

He headed for the station where he knew he would find one of those awful vending machines. He used seventy-five pence for a watery, but warm chocolate drink. Now he had eight pence left.

He sat down on one of the hard plastic chairs and closed his eyes. He had hardly slept at all last night, on the floor of James' room in the Hall of Residence. And he'd had to sneak out first thing as unauthorised visitors weren't allowed. He wished he'd thought to ask James for a loan but at the time he had been too intent on showing he wasn't worried about a thing.

★ ★ ★

When Philip Milligan bought Courockglen House he had known he had found a gem. He had finally moved in on April the first, but it had been no April Fool. This was the place he was going to settle, to review the one or two successes he'd had recently, and to work on a book to follow on from his last television series. He had been determined to brook no interruptions to this schedule so he really didn't know how it was he found himself on a visit to his sister.

His sister! Philip and Alison had never got along. She was twelve years his elder and had always seemed more like a second, extra fussy mother than a sibling. Or perhaps it had been that she had been the perfect child in every way whereas he, until he had broken into television, had never quite seemed to do anything right.

He almost groaned as he pulled his Freelander into the beautifully paved driveway of his sister's house. It was on one of those exclusive little housing estates that had sprung up around Manchester, perfect, expensive, five-bedroomed detached houses somehow shoe-horned into the tiniest of gardens. Everything was manicured and tidy and looked like something out of a magazine. For Philip, a professional historian, the fake Corinthian pillars and the pseudo-leaded windows were painful to behold.

Alison appeared at the door before he had even climbed out of the car. Her brown bobbed hair was as neat as ever and her slacks and shirt were pristine. The carefully applied make up did not, however, hide the ravages of her face.

He air-kissed her cheek and said brightly, 'You're looking well.'

'Thank you for coming. I was expecting you half-an-hour ago but I expect the traffic was bad . . . ?'

Philip immediately felt defensive. He could have phoned her on his mobile, but it hadn't occurred to him. He didn't think they had agreed on an exact time. He bit back an apology and followed her into the shiny white kitchen.

'I'll call Amelia down to say hello in a moment,' she said, reminding Philip of the existence of his niece. She was such a quiet little thing it was easy to forget her. 'But I thought we should have a little chat first.'

It was then that the first real feeling of foreboding touched Philip.

'You have done this kitchen nicely,' he said at random. He had only visited this house a couple of times before but he was fairly sure she had redecorated. He remembered that Alison liked to redecorate.

'It works well, doesn't it?' she agreed with a small, pleased smile. 'I wanted somewhere calm and I think the different shades of white are just what I needed.'

'Ah. Yes. And how is Colin? Is he home at the moment?' Colin was Alison's husband, whose work in the oil-rich countries of the Middle East funded this comfortable lifestyle.

'He came home briefly last week, but he's away again now. He was lucky to get leave at short notice.'

Alison placed a white porcelain teapot on the breakfast bar along with two delicate white cups and saucers. Philip would have preferred coffee, and something to eat, but didn't say so.

'And how are you?' he said, perching uncomfortably on one of the shiny stools. He knew he would have to ask sometime. 'What was it you wanted to talk to me about?'

Alison stirred her tea and didn't look at him. Normally she was alert for his every word and expression, ready to advise or criticise. Her reticence only increased his unease.

She said to the floor, 'I've not been well. How shall I put it? Women's problems, you know.' She gave a little laugh. 'Colin came home last week in order to come to the specialist with me.' Philip jerked his head in surprise and she said quickly, 'It's not serious, don't worry. I mean, it's not life-threatening. But they've decided they do need to operate. It's quite a major procedure. I'll be going into hospital on Monday.'

This was the last thing Philip had expected. Alison was not only always organised, she was also always annoyingly healthy. 'I'm sorry . . . '

'Originally they were going to operate the following week so I thought I had more time to arrange things. But now they've brought it forward. I suppose I should be pleased. I've been in some pain and, well, you don't want to talk about that. I'll be in hospital for up to two weeks and then there'll be quite a lengthy period of convalescence. Colin's plan is that I should go out to Dubai to rest and recover.'

'I suppose that makes sense,' said Philip doubtfully.

'The only difficulty is, of course,

what we should do about Amelia. There is no one to look after her here whilst I'm in hospital, and it won't be ideal for her in Dubai whilst I convalesce.' She gave him a quick glance. She really looked exhausted and Philip felt the stirrings of sympathy.

Then she continued, 'It was Colin who thought of you. As you know, both sets of Amelia's grandparents are no longer with us, and with Colin's sister living in Australia, I was at my wits' end. But Colin remembered you weren't gallivanting all over the country any more. He thought that now you'd settled down this might be an ideal opportunity for you to get to know your niece better.'

Philip felt as though someone had struck him. To get to know his niece better meant . . . what? 'I'm sure Amelia is a very nice girl,' he said faintly, trying to deflect what he knew was coming.

'She is. She's a good girl. She'll be no trouble. And you're the only family she has left in England. It makes sense that she goes to you.'

'Scotland,' said Philip, shaking his head. 'I live in Scotland.'

'Exactly. And you've got that lovely big house, you won't have any difficulty accommodating her.'

'But, Alison,' said Philip, trying to marshal his thoughts and put up a convincing argument. 'What about, about, er, school? And I'm very busy on this book I'm writing. And how will a little girl feel about being whisked off to the back of beyond? Alison, isn't there someone else?'

Alison shook her head very slowly, as if even that was too much effort. 'No, there's no one else. It's the summer holidays just now so we don't need to worry about school. And at seven it wouldn't really matter if she missed a few weeks. What matters is that she has someone to look after her.'

'Couldn't Colin come home?'

'Colin will lose his job if he takes any more time off. His employers pay well, but they're not very understanding. I'm not asking much, Phil. It would just be a month or two.'

'A month or two!'

'Please, Phil.' Alison put out a hand to touch his. Her skin was dry and almost translucently white. She looked so frail that Philip was afraid to argue with her. He felt if she had to make too much effort she might just collapse.

'Well I suppose I could think about it . . . '

'Thank you. I knew I could count on you. I'll call Amelia down, shall I, and then we can sort out the details?'

★   ★   ★

Rachel was making a cake when the policeman phoned. There were hundreds of more important things she should be doing but her mother had taken it into her head that they couldn't welcome her father home without a cake, and as she was clearly too tired and worried to do it herself, the task had fallen to Rachel. She didn't mind. She enjoyed baking and thought this might be a useful first step in encouraging her mother to leave things to her.

She was enjoying the smell of the coffee-flavoured mixture and the feel of the wooden spoon in her hands when the telephone rang. She had persuaded her mother to have a lie down and hurried to pick it up before it disturbed her.

'This is Sergeant McFarlane,' said a deep voice. 'I have a Mr Anthony Collington here. He has given me this number to contact his mother, Mrs Maggie Collington.'

Rachel's first feeling was relief. She had persuaded her mother that it really wasn't anything to worry about, if an eighteen year old didn't turn up for a few hours after a rock concert, but the longer the silence lasted the more concerned she had become.

'Is he all right?' she asked quickly.

'To whom am I speaking?'

31

'Rachel Collington, his sister.' Already the relief was fading into concern. Why on earth were the police phoning? 'Is he in trouble? What's happened?'

Rachel could hear Anthony's voice in the background, arguing to be allowed to speak. That was a good sign, as it meant he was well enough to argue.

The man succeeding in keeping the phone from Anthony. He said ponderously, 'I was hoping to speak to Mrs Collington.'

'My mother isn't here at the moment,' said Rachel. 'I'm Anthony's older sister. Perhaps I can help?'

'We're at the police station in Boroughbie. Perhaps you could come here? Then we can explain what it is all about.'

'You're holding Anthony at the police station?' Rachel almost dropped the phone in her alarm. 'What has he done? Goodness . . . '

'Are you able to come here?'

'Yes. Yes, of course. I'll be there in fifteen minutes.'

It was fortunate she hadn't yet put the cake in the oven. She pushed the mixing bowl to one side and hoped that she wouldn't be away too long. Then she dashed to the little downstairs toilet and washed her hands and checked her appearance. It was a good thing she did so. The floury smudge on her forehead would not have impressed a policeman. Then she scribbled a note to her mother and departed.

Rachel tried to make sense of the phone conversation as she drove her little car along the winding country road. Boroughbie was where she would have expected Anthony to phone from, if he had got the train back from Glasgow and didn't want to wait for one of the infrequent buses that passed their cottage. Why the police were involved she couldn't fathom. But she knew that she had to sort it out before her parents heard. They had more than enough to worry about.

A burly policeman led Rachel through to a small room to the rear of the police station. Anthony was sitting on a plastic chair, wearing a disgruntled expression, shoulders hunched. Rachel gave him a brief hug. 'I'm so pleased to see you,' she whispered.

Anthony said nothing.

The policeman cleared his throat. 'We brought young Mr Collington here as there has been a difficulty with the payment, or rather non-payment, of a train fare.' He sounded deeply disapproving.

'Anthony didn't pay his train fare?'

'That's right. A very serious matter. Something we're trying to crack down on.'

'Yes, of course,' said Rachel, eyeing her brother.

'My wallet was stolen,' he said. 'I tried to explain to them.'

'Theft of a wallet is also a very serious matter. If you had reported that to the police in Glasgow none of this need have happened.'

The man spoke ponderously, but from the glance he cast in her direction

Rachel suddenly realised he wasn't as angry as his words might have indicated.

'I'm sure Anthony is very sorry it has happened, aren't you Anthony?' she said encouragingly.

'Of course I am,' said her brother. He glared at the policeman. 'I've said so twenty times already, haven't I?' Rachel wished he had tried to sound a little more remorseful.

Fortunately, after more disapproval from the policeman, and further explanation and a muttered apology from Anthony, an agreement was reached that the fine would be paid but no charges pressed. Rachel suspected this was the outcome the police had wanted all along. The matter of an unpaid rail ticket was to be viewed as silliness rather than malicious theft. Rachel impressed on him how seriously she took the incident, mixing dismay and anger in her tone, and assured him that it wouldn't happen again.

She couldn't understand why Anthony

had done this. Why hadn't he just phoned? She really didn't think a flat mobile battery was reason enough. 'Haven't you heard of making reverse charges calls from a phone box?' she demanded. From the blank look on his face, clearly he hadn't. Rachel might only be seven years his elder, but technology had moved on a great deal since she was a teenager.

She paid the cost of the ticket, paid the fine and did her best to placate the disapproving police officer. It would have been nice if Anthony had shown a little more contrition, but he merely looked sulky. She sighed deeply as she finally drove away with him in her car.

'I can't believe you did that,' she said.

Anthony hunched his shoulders and looked gloomily out of the side window. He seemed very tall all of a sudden although still slightly built. 'You won't tell Mum, will you?' he said in an undertone.

'No, I won't tell Mum. Or Dad. But Anthony, you real need to sort yourself out. You're eighteen, you need to grow up.'

He said nothing and with an effort Rachel managed to hold her tongue. She hoped that he was sorry and embarrassed about what had happened and that he was just having problems expressing himself.

One thing was clear. It wasn't just her parents who needed Rachel to take a hand in their lives. Anthony most certainly needed it too. What a good thing she had come home.

An Accident Occurs

After the excitement of the afternoon Rachel was very pleased the rest of the day passed quietly. Her mother was rejuvenated by her nap and in the evening the two of them went to the hospital to visit her father. He was sitting up in bed, rather pale but very jolly.

'Lovely to see you, my dear,' he said when she bent to kiss his cheek. Rachel felt a lump in her throat. It was lovely to see him, too, but he seemed rather wan, with the newly-plastered ankle balancing gingerly outside the covers.

'Have they said whether you can come home tomorrow?' asked her mother, fussing around, straightening the bed clothes and fluffing the pillows. It reminded Rachel so much of being ill and pampered as a child that she felt another lump forming.

'It's looking hopeful,' said her father heartily. 'They were worried about that temperature I was running yesterday but that's gone down nicely. If it stays that way tomorrow I can come home on Monday.'

'That's excellent,' said Rachel. 'Mum's got everything ready for you and we can't wait to have you back.'

'I hope your mother isn't working herself too hard.' Rachel's father looked anxiously from his daughter to his wife.

'Of course I'm not,' said his wife.

'Now I'm home, she won't need to,' said Rachel firmly. 'Anthony and I will do all the heavy work between us.'

'Does Anthony know this?' said her father with a faint smile.

'I mentioned it to him,' said Rachel. 'And I'm really looking forward to it. You should see the two collies that came in today, Dad. Real darlings. I'm going to take them for a long ramble on the hill tomorrow, they look like the sort who need their exercise. And Anthony has agreed to do a deep clean of the two kennels you were working on when you had your fall, Dad.'

Anthony hadn't agreed willingly to this, but he had been too cowed by his experiences with the police to refuse. Rachel intended to make the most of his acquiescence.

Her mother was quiet on the way home from the hospital. When they got in Rachel made a pot of tea and they took their normal seats at the kitchen table. There was no sign of Anthony.

'It's good Dad's going to be discharged soon,' said Rachel encouragingly. 'He seems to be pulling through very well.'

'Yes.' Her mother sighed softly and patted her curls, a mannerism she had when something was worrying her. Rachel noticed with a pang that the blonde hair, so like her own, was fading now to grey. She didn't want her parents to get any older.

'What is it, Mum?'

'It's the kennels,' said her mother at last. She patted Rachel's arm. 'I know you said you would help and you mean it, but we can't let you take it on. We haven't liked to say, but the business hasn't been as profitable as we had hoped. We wouldn't be able to pay you.'

'I don't expect to be paid,' said Rachel, horrified. 'If I can have my bed and board I'll be more than happy. I've a bit of money put away if I need it, and I can always do supply teaching once the term starts.'

'It's not right,' said her mother, shaking her head sadly. 'It's not what we wanted for you.'

'But, Mum, I'm happy to be home,' insisted Rachel. How could she make her parents understand that she was doing this for herself as well as for them?

'And we're happy to have you,' said her mother, but she still sounded worried. 'The thing is,' she began, and then paused. 'The thing is, we haven't liked to tell anyone, but there have been some problems with the kennels over the last few months.'

'What kind of problems?' said Rachel,

puzzled. 'I thought your bookings were going really well.'

'Up to last year they were. But recently we've had an unannounced inspection from the animal welfare people, and then one or two clients have cancelled. No-one we know well, but it's made us wonder. It's almost as though someone has been putting out rumours about us.'

'No, surely not.' Rachel couldn't believe anyone would wish harm on her warm, hard-working parents. The thought was very upsetting. She had always been sure that everyone knew what lovely people her parents were. 'I mean, who could it be? You haven't upset anyone, have you? And nobody objected when you first started up the business. Why would this happen now?'

'We don't know,' said her mother, shaking her head sadly. 'We don't know anything for sure, but I felt I should tell you. It's been a worry for us, as you can imagine. It's been distracting your father. He's had one or two little accidents lately, and then that bad fall. I'm sure the worry is making him careless.'

'Well, I'm home now,' said Rachel. 'And if anything untoward is going on I'm going to find out what it is.'

* * *

On Sunday Rachel took Bill and Ben, the two collie dogs, for the walk she had promised herself, up the hills. She needed the solitude to mull over her mother's news. It was difficult to believe that someone would be targeting her parents, trying to ruin their business. She was determined to keep her eyes and ears open and do whatever she could to build up the kennels' reputation once again.

The two border collies were gorgeous. Rachel had never seen ones with such thick, soft fur, their chocolate brown eyes so bright. Bill and Ben didn't seem special enough names for them. 'I should address you as William and Benjamin, at the very least,' she said to them, laying a hand on each silky head.

It was wonderful to be out here. Rachel had enjoyed her life in the city and made the most of the galleries, cinemas and theatres it had to offer, but she truly preferred the outdoors. As she climbed higher amongst the rolling green-brown hills, her spirits began to rise. The air was fresh and warm with just the slightest breeze. The half-grown lambs lumbered after their mothers and the peewits and curlews called. She allowed the two dogs to tow her along by their leads and took it all in.

'I wonder if you would like to run free?' she said to them as they climbed the stile over the fence that separated the fields from the high hills beyond. There were no sheep here and she was fairly confident the dogs would not stray far. They were too friendly for that. 'Let's give it a try, shall we?'

She unclasped their leads and turned to watch them chase their tails, madly

capering about in the afternoon sunshine, toppling over each other. They
came back to her immediately she said
a word, pushing their heads against her
hand and wagging their feathered tails.
No danger of them running off at all.

Far below she could see the tiny
shape of her parents' cottage with the
kennels at the rear. In the five years
since the business had opened the
kennels and runs had weathered to fit
in to the landscape around. Her mother
had been keen to plant trees and bushes
so that they did not stand out starkly,
and she had succeeded. The little
huddle of buildings looked great from
here, just what it was, a successful small
business set in this wonderful country-
side. At least, that was what it would be
again, soon.

Rachel was glad to see that Anthony
had appeared from his bedroom and
was once again working on the
cleaning. It was going to take a bit of
effort to keep him to the task, any task,
but she was sure she was up to it. It

would do him good to apply himself. And it was about time he realised he had to contribute to the family, not just take. She wondered if she could find him a job in Boroughbie, to help out Mum and Dad. Something else to think about as she turned again and headed to the higher moors.

It was when she turned back that things went wrong. She decided to take a different route down, turning east through the neater fields of the neighbouring farmer. Here the original large-scale fields had been separated into a smaller patchwork with new barbed-wire fences. The presence of a digger indicated drainage work was in progress. This land was certainly very well cared-for. The grass looked lush after the heather and bracken of the higher slopes and although she couldn't immediately see any livestock Rachel decided it was time to put the dogs back on the leash.

They had enjoyed the wild runs in the windy upper reaches, chasing the occasional hare and numerous imaginary animals. When she called them they turned immediately to caper back. They were such good dogs, she was really impressed. She had always thought collies could be hard work, but these two were a pleasure. Maybe she should get a collie dog herself, when the time came. She smiled at the thought.

At that moment she realised that Ben had somehow got himself stuck on the other side of one of a barbed wire fences. She called a warning to him to stay there until she could find a gate but he seemed desperate to get back to her side. He threw himself over the top most wire with his usual exuberance, just as she shouted, 'No!'

For a moment it looked as though he would make it. He had taken a running jump and certainly had enough energy to fly right over. But somehow that thick coat got caught on one of the barbs and he twisted in mid air, yelped, and then landed with an ungainly crash.

He rose to his feet immediately but Rachel could see that something was wrong. He limped towards her, tongue lolling apologetically.

'Good boy. Come here and let me have a look.' Even as she crouched down Rachel could see the blood dripping on to the grass as he yelped at her touch. He whined and leaned against her and Bill pushed in as well, sensing something was wrong.

Rachel could feel her heart beating erratically, in horror at what she had done. She tried to lift the animal, but he was bigger and heavier than he looked, and he didn't appreciate her effort. Reluctantly, she let him down and he limped along beside her. The journey home was going to take a long time.

Rachel shuddered as the full import of what had happened sunk in. She had allowed one of the precious visiting dogs to injure himself. She would need to take Ben immediately to the vet. Then, once she had a diagnosis, she would have to phone the impatient Mr Milligan and explain what had happened. Her first impression of the dogs' owner was that he wouldn't let this pass without an enormous fuss.

Even as she thought these depressing thoughts an angry voice broke into them. 'Get those dogs off my land! How dare you walk them here! I have young lambs about and if anything should happen . . . '

Rachel turned to face the angry farmer who had appeared over a crest in the hill. She knew his name, Freddy Smith, and had seen him once or twice in the distance. Her parents said he was nice enough but kept himself to himself. He wasn't being very nice now.

'I'm very sorry,' she said, searching the field for the mystery sheep. She still couldn't see any. 'I would never run them loose with livestock around and in any case, as you can see, they're both on the lead.' Not that poor, hobbling Ben could have gone far from here even if he had wanted to.

'They weren't on the lead a few minutes ago, I saw you. And what's happened to that one? He's injured. Can't you look after your animals?'

'It was an accident,' said Rachel faintly, pulling the dogs back towards her. They were too friendly for their own good and desperate to say hello to this stranger.

'I don't want injured dogs on my land. Nasty unpredictable things they are.' The man made a shooing gesture with his hands and the dogs, finally realising they weren't welcome, cowered back against Rachel.

Rachel thought the man was being ridiculous, but she managed to hold her tongue. She apologised again and led the dogs as quickly as Ben could manage on to a nearby lane. It made the walk home somewhat longer, which wasn't good for the collie, but she didn't think Freddy Smith was concerned about that. 'And don't come back!' he shouted after her. 'I'll call the police if you do, so I will.'

Rachel kept her head down and hurried on. It was the worst possible thing to have happened. Somehow, in the same afternoon, she had harmed one of the dogs and upset their nearest neighbour. This wasn't the right way to restore the reputation of the kennels.

★　★　★

By the time she and Ben arrived at the vet's in Boroughbie, Rachel was almost in tears. Her mother's concerned sympathy had only made her feel worse. Anthony had offered to accompany her in the car, which would have been useful, but she needed him to keep an eye on Bill who was not at all impressed at being separated from his brother.

'I'll be fine,' she had insisted, but each mile that passed and each whimper that poor Ben emitted made her wish she had brought him with her to hold the dog. How could she have been such a fool? Poor, poor Ben, what if he was badly hurt?

She wiped her eyes with the back of her hand and tried to concentrate on driving.

The vet practice was not normally open at this time on a Sunday afternoon but her mother had phoned ahead and been assured that someone would meet Rachel there. Sure enough, a jeep was drawn up at the open back door and as she parked her car a man appeared.

He was dressed in cord trousers and an open-necked shirt, with the inevitable Wellingtons on his feet. He was younger than the vets Rachel remembered seeing previously but looked confident and competent, exactly what she needed.

'I'm so sorry to trouble you on a Sunday,' she said.

'Not a problem. I'm just back from a couple of farm visits so your timing is excellent.'

Rachel was sure it wasn't, but smiled her appreciation at his tact. She opened the rear door of the car and tried to persuade Ben to climb out slowly and sensibly. The dog didn't seem to know what sensible was and launched himself joyfully at the stranger, then staggered and winced as his back leg hit the ground.

The vet swooped down and swung the dog into his arms as though he weighed scarcely a thing. 'Not wise to go throwing yourself around like that,' he said cheerfully. 'Let's get you inside and have a look at that leg, shall we?'

The vet introduced himself as Charlie McArthur and chatted easily with her as he lowered the dog on to the examination bench and began to examine the wound. Rachel held Ben's head. He was a well-behaved dog but even he wasn't too keen on someone touching his sore place. He'd far rather have the chance to give it a good lick himself.

'Caught it on barbed wire, did he?' said Charlie. 'It's quite a long cut but not too deep, probably thanks to all this fur. I'll cut a bit of the fur away and clean it up. I don't think it'll need stitches, but we'll see.'

'Let's hope not,' said Rachel. This injury was going to take some explaining to Philip Milligan. Stitches, which would undoubtedly require a general anaesthetic, would be a nightmare.

'I was such an idiot, letting them run loose up there,' she said regretfully.

'Don't worry about it,' said the vet, giving her an encouraging grin. 'It could happen to anyone. Young dogs like this one are so exuberant they're always getting themselves into trouble. Even if you'd had him on a lead what's to say he wouldn't have twisted his leg in a rabbit hole or caught it on a bit of hidden wire? Believe me, I've seen worse injuries than this from the most minor mishap.'

'You're very kind,' said Rachel. She would be a lot more careful in future, but it was nice to hear someone say she wasn't entirely to blame, especially after the way Freddy Smith had spoken to her.

She rather liked this vet with his ruddy wind-blown face and muddy boots. He was part of the solid country life that she was looking forward to joining. It was good to remind herself that not all locals were rude or unfriendly Now, if she could just get through the telephone conversation with Philip Milligan, telling him the not very good news about his dog, she would be able to relax and look forward to the future once again.

Anthony Makes Plans

Anthony was probably glad Rachel had come home. He knew Mum appreciated her help. And he was grateful for her extracting him from the police station, and saying nothing to their parents about his troubles. But he did wish she wasn't so bossy! She'd always had a tendency to tell him what to do and it had become worse since she became a teacher. Why did everyone think he couldn't make decisions for himself?

Actually, he wasn't quite sure what to do just now, but he knew he definitely didn't want to spend one more minute cleaning the kennels. The only way to avoid that was to get out of the house so he set off down the road.

It was sunny again, almost too hot for walking. He realised he hadn't been away from the house for the two days since his almost-arrest. He stretched his shoulders and looked around. It was good to be out, even if he didn't have a clue where he was going. He didn't even have money for a bus fare into Boroughbie, but he meandered along in that direction and hoped something would occur to him.

When he spotted Gemma Smith at the bus stop his heart skipped a beat. Gemma! He hadn't seen her for weeks. Before he left school, a year ago now, the two of them had caught the school bus together every day. They had been friendly in a casual way. It was only when he stopped seeing her so often that he realised how much he liked her.

'Hiya,' he said, offhand, coming to stand beside her. 'Been waiting long?'

'Ten minutes.' Gemma glanced sideways at him and let her straight dark hair fall over her eyes. 'If the bus doesn't come soon I'll be late for work.'

'Have you got a job?' asked Anthony, surprised and impressed. He thought she was still at school and then remembered that, at a year younger than him, she too would have left now.

'Just for the summer holidays. I'm waitressing at the Boroughbie Arms Hotel. I'm hoping to go to Uni in September.'

'Oh,' said Anthony. 'So am I. I mean, I'm supposed to be, but I'm still not sure.'

'Haven't you got a place?' Gemma seemed more at ease as the conversation progressed. Her interest warmed him.

'I'm supposed to be doing Computing in Edinburgh, but now I'm not sure it's the right thing.' Anthony sighed.

'Your results must have been good, to get in to Edinburgh,' said Gemma appreciatively.

'They were OK.' Anthony knew he could have done a lot better if he had tried. 'And how about you? What are you planning to do?'

'Business Studies at Glasgow Caledonian. I've been offered a provisional place, but it all depends on my

Advanced Higher Maths.'

'You'll be fine. You're good at maths, aren't you?' Anthony was pleased he remembered that.

Gemma shook her head nervously. 'I don't know. I just wish we had the results and I could stop worrying.'

Anthony had been in the same position a year ago and sympathised. 'You'll be fine,' he said again, and then, to change the subject because he had hated it when people asked him about his exams, said, 'How does your father feel about you going away?' He didn't know Gemma's father very well, except that he was seriously scary and very protective of his only child.

Gemma pulled a face. 'He's not keen. He says he's pleased and it would have been what Mum would have wanted, but really he'd prefer it if I just stayed at home, but I can't do that for ever, can I?' She looked at him beseechingly.

'No, of course not. Everyone has to branch out.'

'Exactly. That's why I got him to agree to this waitressing job, it's good for him to see me being a bit independent. And look, here's the bus. Thank goodness, I'd almost given up.'

Anthony had forgotten all about the bus. He watched it draw up with disapproval. He had been really enjoying talking to Gemma.

'Are you coming?' she asked as she climbed on board.

'No. I, er, I've just remembered something I've got to do.'

Anthony raised a hand in a casual farewell and turned for home. It was time he did something to sort out his finances, it was ridiculous not even being able to afford a bus fare. And he had just remembered Dad was due home from hospital that afternoon, probably a good idea if he showed his face.

★   ★   ★

Rachel and her mother had worked hard to make the house perfect for John

Collington's homecoming. They set off immediately after lunch on the Monday to collect him, taking her mother's car as it was more spacious for the invalid. There was no room for Anthony as well, but Rachel had hoped he might be there to welcome them when they got back. He hadn't visited their father in hospital since Rachel had taken over his chauffeuring duties.

'Welcome home, dear,' said her mother as her father gently eased himself out of the car. 'It's wonderful to have you back. You see how Rachel has looked after the hanging baskets for you and tidied your raised beds?' She was still chattering excitedly as she led the way inside, trying simultaneously to manage her own walking stick and help her husband with his crutches.

'Let me do that,' said Rachel, hiding a smile at the muddle they were getting themselves in to. 'Mind the step, Dad. Did the physio show you how to get up steps?'

'She did, although I think I could do

with a bit of practise.' Her father sounded a little breathless and was pleased to lower himself into his favourite armchair as soon as they reached the kitchen.

'A cup of tea?' said his wife solicitously. 'I wonder where Anthony is, I thought he would have appeared by now.'

'He must have gone for a walk,' said Rachel, somewhat baffled. Anthony wasn't the sort to go for walks voluntarily. And if he had, he could at least have taken one or two of the dogs with him, but a quick glance out of the window showed her that all were in their runs.

'It is good to be home,' said her father. 'I'll be back on my feet in no time with you two to look after me.'

'We'll make sure you're not back on your feet until you're ready,' said Rachel firmly.

'Have some cake,' said her mother, nodding her agreement. 'Rachel made it for you. Coffee and walnut, it's your favourite.'

'I can see I'm going to have to get used to being bossed around,' said Mr Collington happily.

Rachel heard a sound at the front door. She frowned. It sounded like a car but they weren't expecting anyone.

'Maybe that's Anthony,' said her mother.

Rachel doubted it, but she rose to go and see. She swung open the old-fashioned wooden door and her face fell at what she saw before her. A fancy four-by-four had parked on the gravel and the person she was least looking forward to seeing was climbing out. She had had a very uncomfortable conversation with Philip Milligan the previous afternoon and had been dreading its sequel.

'Hello there,' she said, taking a step and forcing a smile to her lips. 'We weren't expecting you so early, I thought you said this evening . . . '

'I came as soon as I could,' he said shortly. 'I was worried about Ben. Naturally.'

'Of course. I'm pleased to say he's doing very well but do come in and see for yourself.' Rachel hesitated. She had just realised that there was someone else in the car, a very small someone. 'Would you like to bring in . . . ?' She indicated the blonde-haired little girl firmly strapped on to the back seat.

'My niece. No, this won't take long, she won't mind waiting.'

Rachel examined the child doubtfully. She looked neither happy nor unhappy, she just sat docilely as instructed. Philip Milligan had already entered the house so with a wave to the child she hurried after him.

'Mr Milligan has come to collect his dogs,' she said as she followed him in to the kitchen. She and her mother both glanced at her father. They hadn't wanted to worry him by telling him of Ben's accident and now it looked like it would all come out. 'I'll take him straight through, shall I?' She tried to hustle the newcomer through to the conservatory and out into the yard.

'Why, it's Phil Milligan,' said her father delightedly, stopping her in her tracks. 'I am right, aren't I? Goodness, why did no one tell me we had acquired such a famous client?'

'Good of you to recognise me,' said their visitor, pausing reluctantly. He could hardly carry on walking after such a greeting.

Rachel looked at him more closely. She had thought those dark good looks were slightly familiar but she still couldn't place the man.

'Don't you recognise him?' said her father. 'From *Every House Has A History*? Tuesday evenings, BBC2. Excellent programme. I thought you liked your history, Rachel?'

'I usually play badminton on a Tuesday,' said Rachel. She felt such a fool, of course she should have recognised the man.

'That's who you are,' said Mrs Collington. 'I had a feeling I knew you, but we've all been at sixes and sevens this last week. You've made my husband's day, you know, and here he is, just back from hospital. You're one of his very favourite presenters. He's quite a history buff is John.' She smiled fondly at her husband. She seemed to have forgotten the awkwardness surrounding their visitor's dog.

'Wonderful to meet you in the flesh,' said her husband, stretching out his hand to shake. 'Please excuse me not getting up, I've had a little accident with my ankle.'

Philip Milligan returned the handshake and looked down at the bright white plaster cast. 'I'm sorry to hear that,' he said awkwardly. Rachel almost pitied him. Her father had clearly spoilt what had been intended as a very abrupt entry and exit. He smiled briefly and then attempted to regain control of the situation. 'Nice to meet you. Now perhaps I could see Bill and Ben . . . ?'

'Of course, come this way,' said Rachel and ushered him out before her father's enthusiasm could delay them further. 'I'm sorry about that,' she said.

'And about not recognising you before.'

'No reason why you should,' he said huffily.

'And I'm really sorry about Ben. I know I should have taken more care of him, I loved taking him for a walk and I wouldn't have had this happen to him for the world. It's just that he's such a boisterous dog.'

'Nothing like this has ever happened when he's been with me,' said the man pointedly.

Rachel blushed, in mortification at her silliness and at the impatience in the man's voice. She had hoped he might have calmed down a little since that difficult phone conversation, but obviously not.

'I'm very sorry,' she said again, pulling open the gate to the run. 'Here he is. You can see for yourself how he's doing. The vet said it wasn't too bad a cut but he'd like to see him again in a day or two. We'll cover all costs, obviously.'

She paused as Philip dropped to his

knees and embraced both dogs. Bill was as exuberant as ever, but Ben approached with a decided limp and looked very forlorn with his large plastic collar designed to stop him worrying the wound. Philip stroked his head and then gently examined the back leg.

Rachel held her breath. What if he found something she and the vet had missed? What if he was absolutely furious?

'There, boy,' said the man softly, patting the two dogs again and then rising to his feet. 'I'm glad to see the damage isn't any worse than you said.'

'I told you exactly what had happened,' said Rachel indignantly.

'Hmm.' The man didn't sound impressed. Rachel wanted to argue with him, to explain her side of things. But the problem was she had been in the wrong and knew it.

'I'm sorry,' she said for the umpteenth time.

'Yes. Now, let me settle what I owe

you and I'll be on my way.'

'We're not charging you, not after what has happened.'

'That's no way to run a business,' said the man, one dark eyebrow raised. 'I had heard that you were having one or two difficulties and it's not surprising if this is how you go about things.'

'This isn't normally how we go about things,' said Rachel, forgetting she was supposed to be placating. Really, the man was insufferable. 'Ben is the first dog who has ever been injured whilst staying with us. And therefore the first one we are waiving the fee for. And where did you hear we'd been having difficulties?'

'I don't recall offhand,' said the man, unperturbed by her anger. He drew a cheque book from his pocket. He mentioned the amount he had agreed with her mother and began to make out a cheque.

'Mum won't take it,' said Rachel.

'That's up to her.' He tore it off with a flourish and handed it over. 'Now, if you could collect together the dogs' blankets for me, I'll be off. I don't like to leave Amelia alone for long.'

Rachel glared. It was as though he was blaming her for leaving the child in the car, when she had been more than happy to invite her inside. She pushed the cheque into her back pocket, determined not to cash it, and went to do as he asked. The sooner he left, the better.

Her father seemed genuinely sorry that Philip Milligan couldn't stay longer and issued an invitation to call round any time. Rachel didn't think it would be taken up. She walked with him to his car, torn between her annoyance and gratitude that he didn't complain about poor Ben's injury to her parents.

Anthony appeared at that moment and for once he seemed quite elated. She introduced him to Philip who gave a perfunctory nod and drove off.

'Friendly type, isn't he?' said Anthony with a grin. 'Did he make any more fuss about the dog?'

'He wasn't too happy, but I suppose that's to be expected. And he did insist on paying, which Mum and I had agreed we shouldn't expect.'

'Of course he should pay. I bet he's loaded, driving a great big car like that.'

Rachel sighed. She wasn't so worried about whether or not Philip Milligan was 'loaded'. Her concerns centred around the fact that he, too, had clearly heard rumours about Collington Boarding Kennels. 'We need to get more customers,' she said, watching the tail of his car as it disappeared from sight. 'We need to keep our current ones happy and find some new ones. Anthony, have you heard any rumours going round about the kennels?'

'Rumours? No, never. Why should there be any rumours?'

'That's what I don't know.' Rachel shook her head. 'Anyway, come on in and see Dad, it's great to have him home. And don't mention rumours or Ben hurting himself or anything worrying to him, OK?'

Anthony didn't generally give much thought to his parents' business and whether it was or wasn't doing well. He didn't mind walking and feeding the dogs although cleaning them out was the pits. Even this time last year, when he'd been around the house more than he'd planned, he hadn't taken that much interest. He'd had most fun when he visited Rachel in Liverpool and then spent a couple of months with an uncle in France. Home was just home, something he didn't think much about.

Now he wondered if it was true the business was running into difficulties. He decided to pay a bit more attention to the conversations that were going on around him and to his surprise he found that they were fairly interesting. And best of all they gave him an excuse for getting in touch with Gemma again.

The kennels needed more clients. And if they needed more clients then they should do some advertising, obviously. He was determined to help out now. During his last year at school he and Gemma had both participated in a Youth Enterprise Scheme, selling homemade sweets, and together they had designed an award-winning advertising poster. Maybe she would be interested in helping him out with something similar for the kennels. There was no harm in asking, was there?

The next difficulty was how to approach Gemma. He'd never been to her house. His parents insisted Freddy Smith was a perfectly nice man, but Anthony knew he wasn't well liked locally and almost never had visitors. Gemma and her father had moved to the area four years ago, which made them even more recent *incomers* than the Collingtons. As far as he knew the father had never made any effort to mix.

Anthony didn't fancy phoning the house in case he had to speak to Freddy Smith. Then he remembered there was one other place he could find Gemma. He negotiated a loan from Rachel and took the bus into Boroughbie. He had no idea what days Gemma worked but the only way to find out was to go to the Boroughbie Arms Hotel and ask.

For once in his life he was lucky! Gemma was working that very day and the plump and friendly lady at the front desk told him to go through if he wanted to say hello.

Gemma wasn't so happy to see him. 'I'm working,' she hissed at him when he seemed to want to chat.

'But I need to talk to you.'

She frowned. 'I finish at three. I suppose you could order yourself something and wait for me until then.'

Anthony glanced around at the clientele of the little restaurant. They were mostly families and middle-aged tourists and he couldn't see himself feeling at ease. Or able to afford the prices they were paying.

'I'll meet you outside when you've finished.'

'OK. Look, I've got to go.'

The next hour seemed a very long one and Anthony was leaning against the pillars at the bottom of the broad steps of the hotel entrance before the appointed time. Eventually Gemma appeared, still in her waitress outfit of black and white, neat and pretty. It had been worth the wait.

'I don't have long, I've got to get the three-thirty bus.'

'Let me buy you an ice cream and we can sit in the park for a bit.' Anthony had planned this out and was pleased when she nodded. They chose flavours from the locally produced ice cream in the shop beside the hotel and wandered down to watch children on the boating lake.

'Are you enjoying your job?' asked Anthony. It was so good to be with her again.

'It's all right.' She shot him a brief smile that made his heart beat faster. 'Not exactly my life's ambition, but Mrs Mackenzie who runs the hotel is really nice. All the staff seem happy.'

'I could do with a job in a place like that.'

'Mmm. What was it you wanted to talk to me about?'

Anthony was happy to talk to her about absolutely anything. And unless he was reading things totally wrong, she didn't seem to mind being with him. So he broached the subject of the advertising campaign, not mentioning the difficulties the kennels were having just now but explaining they wanted to bring in some new business.

Gemma seemed interested. She nodded and licked the last of the strawberry ice cream from her fingers. 'So are you thinking of posters to put up around town? Or an advert for the paper?'

'Both, I suppose. Although the advert would cost money. And I thought some of those little bits of paper you can hand out to people.'

'Flyers. Yes. We could do those as a small version of the posters.'

'So you'll help?'

'Yes, why not?' Gemma looked down as she spoke but Anthony thought she was pleased. 'It sounds like fun. Come on now, we'd better run or we'll miss the bus. Unless you've something you need to stay in town for?'

'No, I'm coming home too.' Anthony wasn't going to miss the chance to spend extra minutes with her.

'When do you want to start?' she said, once they had found seats on the bus.

'As soon as possible.'

'Can I come to your house? I don't think my dad will be . . . too keen on us working at mine.'

'Of course. We can work on the computer in my room.' Anthony wanted to punch the air, this was going so well. 'We could go back there now, make a start straight away.'

'No, Dad'll be expecting me home. But I could come round tomorrow morning, say about ten?'

'Brilliant. Don't say anything to Mum and Dad about what we're doing. I want this to be a surprise.'

Rachel Pays A Visit

Rachel walked slowly up the winding track towards Courockglen House. It was cool under the shade of the broad-leafed trees and smelt of warm, damp undergrowth. Normally she would have enjoyed the way the sunlight filtered through the greenery, dappling the ground with golden patches, but just now she was too busy chewing her lip and wondering if this visit was a good idea.

She was very sorry about Ben's injury and had apologised to Philip Milligan more times than she could count. The sensible thing to do would have been to phone to check on his progress and then forget the whole incident. But when she mentioned a possible visit, her mother had been delighted with the idea. She seemed to think it was just the thing to mollify

Philip Milligan. Rachel wasn't so sure. The man would probably think her visit an imposition, but she had come so far now she had to go through with it.

And part of her was interested to see the reputedly beautiful old house, tucked away so deep among the rolling hills and woods that you never caught a glimpse of it from the road.

She knew she was nearing the dwelling when the trees were replaced by rhododendrons, and then the drive opened out on to a grassy area. She paused and blinked in the sudden sunlight. The house stood four-square before her, even larger than she had expected, and beautiful in the local grey whinstone with red sandstone around the windows and door.

'Gosh,' she said under her breath. 'This isn't a house, it's a mansion.' She glanced back over her shoulder at the cool tunnel of the driveway, but there was no chance of disappearing unseen. The door to the front porch was open and the dogs had heard her footsteps.

With a volley of barks, they threw themselves towards her.

Rachel walked to meet them, smiling as she bent to acknowledge their welcome. Bill reached her first, pushing his beautiful soft face against her hand, whining with pleasure. Ben arrived more slowly, hampered more by the plastic collar he still wore than any obvious injury to his leg.

'Hello, my darling, how are you?' she said, running her hand along his silky back and gently over his haunches. 'I'm sure you're not supposed to be running about like this. Didn't the vet tell you to try and rest?'

'Not much chance of that when visitors arrive unannounced,' said a voice from the doorway.

Rachel sighed. She knew Philip's welcome would never match that of the dogs, but he could be a little bit more pleasant, couldn't he?

'I'm sorry,' she said, determined to remain good-tempered. 'I hope I haven't caused him to do anything silly.'

'No more than he's been doing since we got home,' said the man grimly. 'I've tried to keep him inside but with the weather so sultry we've had the doors open and any excuse and he's off . . . ' He bent and patted the dog. 'You're an idiot, aren't you? But then we've always known that.'

Rachel smiled more genuinely, seeing his affection for the great soft beast.

'I just wanted to pop by and see how he was doing,' she said, deciding it was best to explain her presence. 'It's good that he's so bright in himself. I hope the cut is healing all right.'

Philip tossed back the dark hair and considered her for a moment. She wondered if he was going to remind her it was no thanks to her if it did heal fine. Instead he said after a pause, 'That's very kind of you. Would you like to come in for a cup of tea?'

Rachel was stunned. 'Oh, no, I don't want to trouble you. I was just popping by . . . '

'Have you walked all the way here?

That's not just 'popping by'.'

'I like to walk,' said Rachel simply. She gestured to the trees and the hills beyond. 'Especially here. It's lovely, isn't it?'

'Very. It's also rather warm and I'm sure you could do with some refreshment. Do come on in.'

'Well . . . ' Rachel was pleased to be invited, but she still wasn't sure how she felt about this man. His moods could change all too quickly.

Ben nudged her leg and Philip said, 'See, Ben wants to see a bit more of you.' There was the sound of a child's voice from the house and his mouth became a grim line again. 'And you can come and say hello to my niece, Amelia. Perhaps you'll know how to talk to her.'

Rachel was interested now and followed him inside without further protest.

She barely had time to take in the polished wood of the porch and the coloured glass of the secondary front door before they were in the gloom of a large hall. It was degrees cooler in here and Rachel felt she had taken a step back in time. The walls were panelled, the floor tiled in a complicated pattern.

Then the child's voice could be heard again, and this time Rachel realised it was a cry.

'Oh, no, what has she done now?' said Philip, hurrying through another door at the rear of the hall that took them into a massive kitchen. A tiny blonde girl was standing beside the white sink, trying to rinse her hand but yelping every time the water touched her.

'Amelia! What happened?' Philip rushed forward and then stopped before he reached the child, as though unsure what to do next. He put out a hand and then dropped it to his side.

'I cut myself,' said the girl in a whisper.

'For goodness sake! What were you doing with a knife? You should have asked . . . '

'Let me have a look,' said Rachel calmly. Shouting was the very last thing the youngster needed. She was in shock and wanted reassurance.

She put one arm around the child's shoulders and gave her a slight hug, and then took the injured hand in her own. Blood was welling up along the edge of a cut, but when she rinsed it under the tap the bleeding slowed. After a further rinse it had almost stopped.

'Not too much to worry about,' she said cheerfully. 'Nothing like the mess Ben got himself in to, you'll be glad to hear. Now, if I could have a clean tissue for you to hold over it for a while . . . ?' She looked at Philip who looked blank. 'Or kitchen towel, perhaps?'

'Yes, yes, of course.' He hurried to bring her what she required and watched in silence as she settled the child in a chair at the long wooden table. Then he cleared his throat, seeming to realise that some comment was called for. Rachel smiled to herself. It was strange to see the confident television personality at a loss for words before a small child.

'I'll, er, put the kettle on for that tea, shall I?'

'That would be good,' she said encouragingly. 'Perhaps your niece would like a cup, too? With sugar.'

'I'm not supposed to have sugar in my tea,' whispered the girl.

'It's for the shock, an important medicinal purpose,' said Rachel firmly. 'And now I suppose I should introduce myself, shouldn't I? I'm Rachel and I live not far from here . . . ' She kept up a flow of chatter, partly to soothe the child, but also to give Philip time to collect his wits. And as her father would have said, chattering wasn't exactly a hardship to Rachel.

By the time tea and biscuits were on the table she had spoken of her move home, enthused over the Southern Uplands, petted the dogs, and found out that Amelia was seven years old.

'What a grown up girl you are for seven,' she said encouragingly. 'Is this fruit salad you're making?'

The girl nodded her shiny blonde head. She was small for her age but her eyes were bright with intelligence and she seemed to take in everything Rachel said. The problem was getting her to respond.

'Who showed you how to make fruit salad?'

'My mum.'

'That's very clever. My mum's the one who taught me to cook, too. Preparing food's fun, isn't it?'

The child nodded and took a biscuit. Rachel decided to let her eat it in peace and turned her attention to the uncle who now sat down opposite her. He nodded towards the child. 'Is she going to be all right?'

'She'll be fine. Won't you, Amelia?' The child nodded, silent again. 'How long is she staying with you?' Rachel asked Philip. It seemed an odd arrangement to her. Philip Milligan didn't strike her as very child-friendly.

'A month or so,' he said without

enthusiasm. 'Her mum, my sister, is in hospital having an operation. The op's gone well thank goodness, but it'll take her a while to get over it.'

'It's very kind of you to look after your niece,' said Rachel. She suspected this wasn't something he had taken on willingly and the shrug he gave seemed to confirm this. Poor child. At least he didn't actually put his reluctance into words. 'It's a great place for children here. All the gardens and open space, and the dogs to play with.'

'It's a bit lonely. And Ben's not supposed to be playing just now.' He shot her a meaningful look so she knew he hadn't forgotten whose fault that was.

'I wonder if I can find you any local families with children for her to play with,' mused Rachel. She was sure her mother would know someone suitable.

'We're perfectly all right here,' said Philip abruptly, seeming to take this as criticism.

Rachel sighed. She never could say the right thing with him. 'I'm sure you are. Now I'd better be on my way. Thanks for the tea. Can I have a quick look at your finger, Amelia? That looks fine. I don't think you'll need a plaster unless you're doing something that might get it dirty.' She wondered whether Philip would actually have plasters in the house. It was the sort of thing you kept a supply of if you were used to being around children, which he probably wasn't.

He walked with her to the front door. 'Thanks for calling round,' he said abruptly.

'My pleasure. If you feel like bringing Amelia to visit us, feel free. You know my father would love to see you.'

He nodded but didn't actually agree. What a strange man. Rachel strode off across the gravel. She turned to look back at the house as she reached the entrance to the driveway and found he was still standing at the door, watching her. He raised a hand in farewell. For some reason she blushed as she waved in return.

'Just exactly what do you think you're doing?' demanded a deep voice that was all too familiar to Anthony.

He swung round, immediately guilty although he didn't know why he should be. He and Gemma were just putting up a few posters. The voice belonged to Sergeant MacFarlane as he had known it would.

'We're putting up posters,' he said, trying to be polite. Rachel had gone on and on at him about how being polite made life so much easier.

The policeman folded his arms across his broad chest and shook his head at them.

'Is there a problem?' said Gemma. She sounded scared.

'I don't see why there should be,' said Anthony.

'Yes, there is a problem.' The policeman sighed lugubriously. 'Have you ever heard of fly-posting? It's against the law to put up posters on any property that isn't your own and even on your own property there can be restrictions.'

'But that's ridic ... ' started Anthony, and then thought better of it. 'That's really, er, a shame.' He could feel colour rising to his face and he hated that.

They had put up at least twenty posters around Boroughbie and the plan had been to do the same in Moffat the next day.

'I never thought,' said Gemma, chewing her lip.

'Other people do it,' said Anthony.

'Yes, and if caught they can receive a hefty fine.' The man glowered at them. 'Is that what you want?'

Anthony balked. He still hadn't repaid Rachel for the last fine. 'I suppose we could go and take them all down,' he offered, hoping he could remember where they had put them.

'We're really sorry,' said Gemma. She sounded mortified and that made Anthony feel even worse. He was the one who had got her in to this. It had seemed such a good idea. And the posters were brilliant, they had used a photograph of the kennels around which Gemma had superimposed picture after picture of happy dogs. It was eye-catching and he had been sure it would bring in those much-needed extra few customers.

'I had hoped not to come face to face with you for a while, young man,' said Sergeant MacFarlane, looking Anthony up and down. He didn't seem mollified by their offer or apology and Anthony could feel himself losing his temper.

'Look here . . . '

'What's all this about?' said a new voice.

Anthony had thought his spirits couldn't plummet any lower but he was wrong.

Gemma's father had appeared out of nowhere. Now he was towering over all of them, looking very angry indeed.

'Hi, Dad,' said Gemma, putting a hand quickly on his arm. 'It's nothing.

We were just . . . ' She faltered, which wasn't surprising under the glare her father was giving her.

'Are you in trouble with the police?' he demanded. 'And who is this young man?' He turned his fierce dark stare to Anthony. 'Perhaps you can enlighten me?' he ended, turning to the police officer.

'Certainly,' said the police officer, his tone noticeably more pleasant. 'I was just having a chat with these young people, pointing out they shouldn't be putting up any posters in public places.' Now he made it sound as though it was a very minor misdemeanour.

'So we're stopping right now,' said Gemma quickly, trying to pass the rest of the posters to Anthony. 'Did you come to give me a lift home? That was really kind, but I could have got the bus, Dad.'

'I had to come in to town to see the seed merchant. Thought I'd keep an eye out for you. I didn't expect to see you with a young man and certainly not being accosted by a police officer.'

'We were just having a wee chat,' said Sergeant MacFarlane and Anthony shot him a grateful smile. Maybe the police weren't so bad after all.

'Shall we go?' said Gemma to her father.

Anthony felt he should do something to help her, but he wasn't sure what. She seemed desperate to leave.

'Not until you've introduced me to your friend.'

'Oh, this is Anthony. I know him from school.'

'Anthony?' The man frowned. On Gemma the dark eyes were lovely, but on her father they were definitely scary. 'That wouldn't be Anthony Collington, would it? From the kennels? I thought I recognised you. I should have known. You're nothing but trouble, your family. Just keep away from me and my daughter, do you hear me? Just keep away.'

He took the remaining papers from his daughter's arms and thrust them at

Anthony so suddenly that more than half of them spilled across the pavement. Anthony gathered them as best he could, not helped by the stiff breeze. By the time he rose to his feet again Gemma and her father had gone.

★ ★ ★

Rachel and her parents were at the kitchen table going through future bookings when Anthony appeared. He had been very pleased with himself when he went out that morning, but now he looked thunderous.

'Hello dear, how are you?' said her mother.

'What's happened?' demanded Rachel, and then wished she hadn't. Her parents didn't seem to have noticed anything was wrong. She should have let Anthony slide off to his room and gone looking for him later.

'Is something wrong?' asked their father, turning slowly to examine his son. 'What is it, son?'

'Nothing,' said Anthony, looking desperately from one to the other of them. For all his height and deep voice he looked like nothing so much as a young boy in trouble.

'Do you want a cup of tea?' said Rachel brightly.

'Come and sit down and tell us about it,' said her father.

Anthony hesitated and then slumped down on to one of the chairs. He slapped down a pile of papers that he had been holding under his arm. 'It's these.'

Rachel and her parents leant forward to look more closely. They were posters advertising Collington Kennels, bright and quirky and just the sort of thing they needed.

'But they're brilliant!' she said, surprised. 'Did you make them?'

'Yes, with Gemma Smith. That's what we were doing the other day.' Anthony looked slightly mollified by her praise.

'What a good idea,' said his mother.

'So what's the problem?' asked John, still with his eye on his son.

Anthony shrugged. 'We were putting a few up around Boroughbie and apparently you're . . . not supposed to. We were told to take them all down.'

'Oh, what a shame,' said Maggie sympathetically.

'You should have discussed it with us first, surely you realise you can't put up posters just anywhere,' said Rachel.

'I do now. So I'll just put the whole lot in the bin, shall I?' Anthony looked furious again and Rachel wished her tone had been less critical.

'Absolutely not,' said his father pleasantly. 'They're excellent, we just need to find the right places to put them. Vets' practices, as your mother said, and maybe that notice board at the newsagents.'

Rachel managed to bite her lip and not say anything else critical. The posters were very good and publicity was exactly what they needed to get the bookings up to a reasonable level once again. She wondered who it was that had stopped Anthony putting up the posters, but decided to wait until they were alone before she asked him.

The opportunity to ask never seemed to arise which she regretted strongly a couple of days later. She picked up a copy of the twice-weekly local Gazette on a trip into Boroughbie and was paging through it as she chatted to her mother over coffee when the article caught her eye.

Local Business Adds to Litter Problem. The Gazette's ongoing campaign against litter in our towns seems to have made no impression on local business Collington Kennels, whose posters and leaflets were left strewn about the streets . . .

'Oh no,' Rachel didn't need to read further to know this was not the sort of publicity they had been hoping for. She made as if to turn the page so that her mother wouldn't see the offending article, and then realised there was no chance of keeping it from her parents who both read the paper from cover to cover. And even if she 'lost' the paper one of their friends was bound to mention it. She pushed the paper over to her mother with a sigh. 'Look at that. Just what we didn't need at the moment.'

She hated to see the way her mother's face crumbled as she read. Things had been so much better the last few days, her father definitely on the mend and her mother starting to relax. And now this.

She showed it to Anthony when he came downstairs. He would have to know sometime. For once she felt sorry for him. He had been trying to help, it was such a shame it had turned out so badly.

'But we didn't leave any litter!' he said heatedly. 'I tried to collect everything, really I did. I don't know where they got that from.'

'Maybe you dropped one or two by accident,' said his mother placatingly.

'If only the paper hadn't started this

stupid campaign,' groaned Rachel.

'It's a very laudable campaign,' said her mother.

'Gemma had the leaflets in her bag,' said Anthony, remembering. 'I should have got them back off her. What was she doing throwing them away?'

'She wouldn't do it on purpose. She's such a nice girl.' Rachel wondered, not for the first time, if her mother ever said anything negative about people.

'It's the last time I involve her in anything,' said Anthony, jumping to his feet. 'And don't worry about me causing you any more trouble because I won't. Everything I do goes wrong, so I won't do anything.'

He stormed out of the room and Rachel and her mother exchanged a silent look.

'I'll talk to him later,' said Rachel.

'He's a good boy really,' said her mother.

★ ★ ★

Rachel's move back to the family home hadn't started as well as she had hoped, but she tried to concentrate on the positive. Her father was recovering nicely. All the local vet practices had been happy to take Anthony's posters and a couple of new bookings had come in, possibly as a result. The weather was beautiful and she was enjoying the opportunity to be outdoors. Her parents seemed to think she was doing too much but what they didn't realise was that Rachel needed to be doing something. She revelled in it. It was a pity Anthony wasn't a bit more like her, but she was working on that.

It was a Wednesday morning, a week or so after her visit to Philip Milligan's house, and she was out walking once again, this time with two of the visiting dogs, sensibly on their leads. One was a slightly loopy collie-cross and one a highly strung springer spaniel so leads were definitely a good idea. She let the dogs drag her up the track over the hill to the east, away from Freddy Smith's land, and then dropped back down to the road to do a circuit home.

As she approached the road a little white van came around the corner going rather too fast. The brakes squealed as the driver realised how close he was to the verge and the van swerved then righted itself and accelerated away. Rachel shook her head. Some youngster, no doubt. You didn't often see driving like that out here. She'd have to make sure she kept the dogs close to her on the grass verge, she didn't want anything to happen to them.

A moment later she heard another loud screech of brakes and this time, if she wasn't mistaken, it was followed by a bang. She began to run in the direction the van had been heading, the dogs more than happy to accompany her.

As she rounded the corner she saw the white van, stationary now and slewed across tarmac. A red car that had obviously been travelling in the opposite direction was stopped so close that Rachel could only assume the two vehicles had hit. She pulled out her mobile and was dialling 999 even as she hurried forward. She gave the location and was able to report that nobody seemed to be hurt. Certainly the two drivers were already climbing out of their cars and launching into a heated exchange.

'Women drivers!' shouted the man who had been driving the van. He was older than Rachel had expected, a heavy-set man in his fifties. 'What were you doing on my side of the road? Never look where you're going.'

'I wasn't on your side of the road,' said the woman, far more quietly. She was Rachel's age or a little older and looked very shaken. 'And I wasn't driving too fast, either, which you certainly were.'

'Are you both all right?' asked Rachel dropping her phone back into her pocket.

The man had opened his mouth to

launch into another tirade but paused when he saw her. He glanced quickly up and down the road. 'Yes, ah, fine, no problem. If this little lady will just move her car out of the way I'll be getting on.'

Rachel was close enough now to see that the cars had touched, but only slightly as they had both swerved. The bumper of the red car was dented. Rachel peered inside and was relieved to see that there were no passengers. Likewise in the van, although she could see a cage in the back which might have held a dog.

'I'll need to take your name and phone number, contact details,' said the woman, shaking her head to clear it. 'My car's damaged, my insurers will want to contact yours.'

'It should also be reported to the police,' said Rachel. She was beginning to feel angry on the woman's behalf. The accident could have been far worse. She was glad she had already called the emergency services, clearly this man had no intention of doing so.

'No need for that,' said the van driver, just as she had expected.

'I'll just get my handbag, I think I've got a pen in there,' said the woman, but she didn't move. Instead she put her hand against the bonnet of the car and swayed slightly.

Rachel jumped forward. 'You need to sit down,' she said, trying to support the woman and not get tangled in the dogs' leads. The dogs had been trying to make friends with these strangers but now they seemed more interested in whatever was in the van.

Rachel pulled them over and got the woman to sit on the grass verge. 'Put your head between your knees,' she said. She wasn't sure if the woman was actually going to faint but better to be safe than sorry.

She turned back to the man who had closed the door of his van and was glaring at her dogs. 'I need to get going,' he said. He indicated the woman with a jerk of his head. 'Can you get her to move her car?'

'Not right now,' said Rachel firmly. 'I don't suppose you've got one of those traffic triangles in your car have you? You're stopped a bit close to this corner and we don't want the next car that comes round to hit you both.'

'Traffic triangle?' he said blankly.

'I have,' said the woman faintly. 'It's in the boot.'

Rachel went to fetch it, still towing the reluctant dogs behind her. Once she had put the sign out to warn any approaching traffic of a hazard ahead she felt a bit calmer. The road in the other direction was straight so any vehicles would see them and be able to slow in time.

'I really need to get going,' said the man. He was assessing the two cars and Rachel guessed he was trying to see if he could get past if he reversed his. She wouldn't put it past him to drive away and leave the two of them. Fortunately, there didn't seem to be enough room.

'I'll get my bag in a minute,' said the woman. Colour was coming back to her face. 'Sorry about this.'

'I don't think you're the one who needs to be sorry,' said Rachel, and then was distracted by a volley of barks from the back of the van. 'You've got a dog in there,' she said to the man, unnecessarily.

'Aye. So?'

'Don't you think you should check it's all right? You must have had to brake pretty hard.'

'It'll be fine,' he said, making no move to open the door.

Rachel was standing near the back of the van and peered in through one of the little windows. As far as she was concerned, it was worrying that the dog had only just started to bark. Was it, too, in shock?

As her eyes adjusted to the gloom she saw a small Westie in the metal dog cage. The dog was shaking and very definitely unhappy. Without another thought she opened the rear door and bent to have a closer look.

'Hey!' shouted the man, rushing to

her side. 'I'm not having this. Interfering busybody . . . '

The dog quietened as she saw Rachel
and put her nose to the bars of the
cage. The Westie rose on her back paws
and greeted her through the bars and
Rachel put out her fingers, not quite
touching, but showing she was friendly.
The little dog was a beauty, well
groomed and in excellent condition.

'See, she's fine, leave her be,' said the
man, trying to pull her back so he could
close the door.

'I know that dog,' said Rachel slowly.
She leant closer, trying to see if there
was a name tag.

'No you don't. That's my dog.' The
man pulled her roughly this time but
Rachel was angry now and shook
herself free.

'That's Jinty,' she said in disbelief. 'I
know her owners. They're very protective of her. What on earth is she doing
here?'

'You've made a mistake. She belongs
to a friend of mine,' said the man,

changing his story. He moved forward and the dog shrank back. That was enough for Rachel.

The driver of the red car had come to stand behind them and she hastily handed over the leads of the other two dogs. 'Hold these will you?' She reached forward to open the cage. 'Here Jinty girl, come on now.'

At the sound of a familiar voice the little dog crawled forward, almost on her stomach, still eyeing the man fearfully. Rachel whisked her into her arms and held her close. The dog wore no collar but there was no mistaking her beautifully trimmed coat and gleaming eyes.

'Give her back,' said the man, making a grab for the animal.

'Oh no, you don't,' said the woman, now apparently fully recovered. Rachel took advantage of the distraction to step away and the woman continued, 'I don't think that is your dog at all. In fact, I think you have dog-napped her. I happen to know that quite a bit of this has been going on in the area recently. In fact I've been researching it for my job.' She had found her handbag now and produced a notepad and pen. 'Now what do you have to say about that?' she said expectantly.

For once in her life Rachel was speechless and had never been so glad to see another car as she was when the police car drew up behind her.

★ ★ ★

'You're famous,' said Anthony with something between a grin and a sneer. 'Quite the local heroine.'

Rachel groaned. 'How was I to know she was a journalist? I would have been more circumspect if I'd realised.'

'Excellent publicity for the kennels,' said her father, massaging his leg just above the plaster. 'And Mr and Mrs Johnston are delighted, they can't say enough in your praise.'

'I'm just glad I got Jinty back for

them.' Rachel shuddered. 'You know they think the man was heading for the ferry at Stranraer? If he'd got across to Ireland they might never have seen her again.'

Philip Makes A Bad Impression

Philip Milligan liked to be right about things, but sometimes it would be easier if he wasn't. Looking after Amelia was just as inconvenient as he had feared. It wasn't that the child was troublesome in herself — quite the opposite, in fact. Most of the time she was good as gold. It was just that he was all too aware he was supposed to be looking after her. There was only so much television she could be allowed to watch, and there weren't many games a seven-year-old could play alone either inside or outside.

In retrospect it might have been a good idea to take up Rachel Collington's offer of an introduction to local children. At the time however, he had been too set on proving he didn't need her advice. She was a rather bossy young woman despite her fairy-like appearance. And she made mistakes, too, look what happened to Ben when she was in charge of him. Although he had to admit the dog wasn't badly hurt, and the woman did have a lovely way with both animals and children.

He sighed. Amelia shot him a worried glance. That decided it for him. The child shouldn't be that anxious, he wasn't really an ogre.

'Would you like to phone your mum in a little while?' he said. Alison had been flown over to Dubai a few days earlier and appeared to be doing well.

The child nodded.

'Good, we'll do that. Then how about a visit to the Galloway Country Fair? It takes place not far from here and they have lots of things to see, archery and birds of prey displays and . . . other things.' Philip had seen the advert in the local paper and it had looked as though it might be interesting. It wasn't his normal sort of pastime, but maybe it would be good for him to take an interest in country pursuits, now he was living out here.

Amelia looked confused rather than enthusiastic, but he felt proud of himself for making this decision. They would have fun. He would make sure they did.

'Can we take Bill and Ben?' she asked quietly. That was the one real plus of her visit, the way she had bonded with the dogs.

'I don't see why not, as long as we keep them on the lead. You can hold one if you want.'

The child's smile was genuine this time.

The good weather was holding and the Country Fair was packed with a mixture of what Philip thought of as 'real' country people in their tweeds, farmers with their open-necked shirts and ruddy faces, and rather too many tourists. There was so much to see that Amelia was flagging before they were half way round. He bought her an ice-lolly and they paused to watch a man demonstrating the handling of ferrets.

Philip hadn't realised what impressive little creatures these were.

'Do you like them?' he said to Amelia, who was watching avidly.

'Yes. They're cute.'

'Don't get too keen, I can't see your mother letting you have one.' Philip had meant this as a joke, but the child's face fell. She hadn't really been thinking of getting one, had she?

The demonstrator brought over a pure white female, known as a jill, to let the audience touch her. Philip had to admit she was a beauty.

Amelia leaned over to stroke the soft head, giggling as the animal nuzzled her. She was so distracted she forgot the rather expensive ice-lolly she had been holding and it fell to the ground.

'Oh no! I hadn't finished it.'

'Never mind, you can't eat it now.'

'But I wanted it.' The child's lip began to quiver and Philip sighed.

'You should have been more careful, shouldn't you? Although I think Ben's quite pleased you weren't.' He gave the collie a nudge out of the way so that Bill could have his share.

'I really liked it,' said Amelia with a sniff.

'Too bad.' Philip was determined not to buy another.

'Hello there,' said a new voice and Philip swung around to see Rachel Collington approaching, accompanied by a man who looked vaguely familiar. She was already crouching down beside the child. 'How are you, Amelia? How's the finger? All healed? That's excellent.'

'Hello,' said Philip, trying not to sound as disgruntled as he felt. Amelia had cheered up immediately she saw Rachel.

Rachel rose to her feet. 'Hello, nice to see you both again. I think you know Charlie McArthur, don't you? He's the vet who's been looking after Ben.'

Of course, that was why he looked familiar. Philip shook hands with the man who previously he had found very pleasant. Now, for some reason, he was irritated by his presence.

'How's Ben doing?' asked the other man, patting the dog's head.

Philip was surprised he could tell the two apart, not many could and Ben was no longer limping. 'He's fine, thanks. No lasting damage.'

'Thank goodness,' said Rachel and pulled a face. 'I'm so sorry it happened . . . '

'Yes, so you've said.' Philip didn't know why he was being so abrupt, he had long since forgiven her.

'Any new television programmes in the offing?' asked the vet, seemingly oblivious of the atmosphere. 'I was quite a fan of your last one, makes you think, doesn't it, how much history there is all around?'

Philip couldn't help but be flattered. 'I'm glad you liked it. We're considering a new series later in the year, but just now I'm working on a book.'

'Fascinating. Same kind of subject?'

'Yes. I'm writing about a couple of the houses we researched, and also showing people how they can do their own researches. What architectural and landscape clues to look out for, where to find land records, that kind of thing.'

'I'm impressed you find the time to do anything, with your niece staying,' said Rachel. 'Although I have to say she's very well behaved, aren't you, sweetie?'

Philip was torn between admitting it was a struggle to work just now and the desire to show what a good uncle he was.

'Uncle Philip lets me watch lots of television,' said the child, immediately debunking that myth. 'Much more than I'm allowed at home.'

'A little television isn't a bad thing,' said Rachel cautiously.

Philip felt criticised. OK, so he didn't know much about children, but he was well aware that too much television was frowned upon. But he was doing his best, wasn't he? He took the child's hand.

'We'll be on our way,' he said. 'We want to look at the, er, tents over here, don't we, Amelia? Nice to see you. Goodbye.' He strode off, trying not to notice the hurt look on Rachel's face. She should stop being so interfering, then he wouldn't have to get annoyed.

He wondered what she was doing here with the vet. Charlie McArthur was perfectly pleasant, just not the right man for Rachel. Not that it was anything to do with him, of course.

*   *   *

Anthony was leaning against the pillars at the entrance to the hotel where Gemma worked. He had checked with the receptionist and knew she finished at four today so if he waited long enough she was bound to appear.

He hadn't seen her for over a week, since the fiasco with Sergeant MacFarlane and her father. Initially he had been too embarrassed and annoyed to want to seek her out, and then he had doubted whether she would want to see him anyway. But he was bored, and he missed her. They had had such fun putting together the posters. Maybe she wouldn't want to speak to him, but he wouldn't know unless he tried.

When Gemma did appear she was accompanied by another girl also in the waitress's uniform. The two were giggling together and Anthony scowled.

'Hiya,' he said, pushing himself away from the wall.

Gemma hesitated and paused. 'Oh. Hi. Were you looking for me?' She looked doubtfully at the other girl.

'I'm just on my way. Mum's picking me up outside the Co-op.'

Anthony relaxed as she moved off. He remembered her vaguely from school. She had been in Gemma's year, rather loud and intimidating.

'I wondered if you wanted to go for a walk or something,' he said, looking at the ground. 'I've got my mum's car. I could give you a lift home after.'

'Well, OK.'

119

They set off down the street towards the park. Anthony was hurt that she didn't seem more keen.

'Was your dad really annoyed about us putting up those posters?' he asked. He suppose he should apologise. It had all been his idea.

'Yeah, he was a bit.' Gemma smiled then, which showed she wasn't too cross with him. 'He's a bit overprotective and I think it gave him a shock, seeing us in trouble with the police.'

'We weren't really in trouble.'

'No. That sergeant was quite nice, wasn't he? He could have been really nasty.'

'He was OK. Shame the whole thing got into the papers though. I don't know how that happened.' He watched her to see how she reacted but she didn't seem guilty.

'I don't know either. I thought we collected everything together and took it home with us.'

'We must have missed one or two. That's no reason to mention the kennels by name in the paper.'

'It was a real shame,' agreed Gemma sympathetically. Then she tossed her long hair over her shoulder and shot him a smile. 'But you got good publicity in the next issue. I saw that article about your sister. Imagine rescuing a dog! She was really clever to recognise it.'

'Lucky to be in the right place,' said Anthony, although secretly he was rather proud of Rachel.

They chatted more easily now, passing the park with its boating lake and on under the old railway line. There was a path that went through the town wood and then looped back past the caravan park and they took this.

'Do you want to go for a coffee?' asked Anthony as they neared the town once again. He was in funds as his parents had paid him for white-washing some of the kennels.

'I better not. Dad'll expect me to get the five o'clock bus which means I'd be home by half past.'

Anthony took a deep breath. He'd only asked out a couple of girls before and that was years ago, when he was a kid of fifteen. 'I was wondering.' He paused, hoping he wasn't going to blush. 'I thought maybe we could go out, you know? Go to a movie or something . . . ' His voice tailed off.

Gemma wasn't looking pleased, or even embarrassed. She was just shaking her head. 'No. I'm sorry, I can't.'

'You can't?'

'My dad'd be furious. It's just been him and me since my mum died when I was ten. Dad doesn't like me to go out much.'

'That's ridiculous.' Anthony was suddenly grateful for his more easy-going parents. 'You've got your own life to live. You said yourself he's going to have to get used to you being away when you go to university.'

'Dad's had a bad time,' she said defensively. 'It's not been easy for him.'

'I don't see why that should stop you having a boyfriend. Unless you're using

122

it as an excuse? You probably don't want to go out with me anyway.'

Gemma sighed and didn't deny this. Anthony realised belatedly that he wasn't doing his case any good by arguing with her.

'I need to get back,' she said.

'I'll give you a lift, like I said. You'll have to take it now, the bus will have gone.'

The journey passed almost in silence and Gemma made him stop just before the entrance to her farm track. She wasn't joking about not wanting to be seen with a boy — or was it not wanting to be seen with him?

★   ★   ★

Rachel couldn't stop giggling as she returned from taking the phone call. This was so preposterous!

'Who was that?' asked her mother. She had been sitting at the kitchen table supposedly doing paperwork, but mostly frowning out of the window at her husband who had insisted on doing a little gardening in the raised beds at the back. Now her attention was caught by Rachel.

'That was the organiser of the Boroughbie Show.' Rachel sank down into a chair and shook her head. The Boroughbie Show was the local agricultural show, a major event every August.

'Barney Johnstone?' asked her mother, who knew all the locals. 'What did he want?'

Rachel grinned. 'He wanted to ask me if I would open the show for them this year.'

Her mother smiled doubtfully. 'You're joking, I presume? I'm sure I heard they'd got that presenter from Border Television coming to do it.'

'They had, but she's just had a bad fall from her horse and has had to pull out. It's very much last minute as the show is a week on Saturday. So for some reason, they thought of me! They must be mad.'

'I'm sure you'd do it very well,' said

her mother loyally. 'But why you?'

'I think it was that whole saga over Jinty. Apparently Sarah Stretton, the journalist who was involved in the crash, is on the organising committee for the show, and she suggested it.'

'Are you going to do it?' asked her mother, still torn between pride in her daughter and surprise that she should be asked. 'Oh, just a moment, your father's trying to lift that bag of peat, I told him he wasn't to do anything that might risk him falling again.' She limped over to the conservatory door and opened it to chastise her husband.

Rachel watched with a smile on her face. Her mum would never stop her dad doing things now he was feeling so much better. Personally she was glad to see him so full of life.

'He's coming in for tea,' said her mother, looking pleased with herself.

'Now, you haven't answered my question — did you say yes?'

'I said I would help out if they were desperate, but only if they really couldn't get anyone else. After all, I'm hardly a celebrity, am I? I'm sure all the farmers won't want to be presented with their prize trophies by someone like me.'

'I don't see why not,' said her mother immediately.

'Well, I suggested they contact a real local celebrity — Philip Milligan. Lots of people know him from the television. So Barney has gone away to make some enquiries.'

'What a shame,' said Mrs Collington. Now she had got over her initial surprise she seemed quite keen to see Rachel thrust into the spotlight. 'You'd look lovely doing it, you're such a pretty girl. And that nice vet Mr McArthur would be bound to see you there which wouldn't do any harm at all.'

'Charlie and I are just friends.'

Mrs Collington ignored that. 'Here's your father. Tell him all about it whilst I make the tea.'

'You tell him. I'll make tea.' Rachel jumped up. She was a little worried about how slowly her mother was moving just now. Her medication had been changed at her last out-patient appointment and this one didn't seem to be working so well. She didn't want to make an issue out of this now but if there was anything she could do to ease the burden, she was determined to do it.

A Panic For Rachel

Philip wasn't sure why he had agreed to help out the organisers of the Borough-bie Show. It wasn't as if agricultural shows were his kind of thing. Yet somehow, when he heard that Rachel Collington had recommended him, he had found himself agreeing to be their guest of honour. With the proviso that Rachel herself should also be involved to help him present all the prizes.

Now he was looking forward to seeing her again. There was no denying that she was bossy and interfering, but she was also — interesting. And the fact that she was very pretty didn't do any harm. He wondered if that rather dull vet would be around, and hoped devoutly that he wouldn't.

It was only when he and Amelia were on their way to the show that he realised he should have given some thought to the child. It wouldn't be much fun for her on her own whilst he was performing his duties. Situations like this were constantly tripping him up. Alison didn't realise how unsuited his life was to looking after a young child. He sighed. One good thing was that Alison was at least truly on the mend. And another was that he and Amelia were no longer quite so shy with each other.

But that didn't solve the problem of what to do with her today. He looked around as they arrived at the show ground. He saw a young man who looked vaguely familiar.

'Don't I know you?' he asked hopefully, and realised immediately that he did. 'Rachel's brother! Of course.' He wished he could remember his name.

'I'm Anthony,' said the youth, smiling faintly as though he realised Philip's predicament. 'And this is Gemma, a . . . friend of mine.'

'Pleased to meet you, Gemma,' said

Philip, shaking hands and giving his most charming smile. 'This is Amelia, my niece. We were just looking for Rachel. And a Mr Johnstone?'

The slim dark-haired girl smiled, but more at the child than at him. 'They're over there,' she said with a wave of her hand, and then turned to the youngster. 'Have you ever been to Boroughbie Show before?'

'No,' said Amelia in her usual faint tones.

'You'll have a good time,' said Philip rallyingly.

'Gemma and I were just going to watch the show-jumping,' said Anthony, making to leave, but Gemma seemed to notice a quiver of interest in the child.

'You could come with us,' she said. 'If you want.'

'I like horses,' said the child.

That decided Philip. These youngsters could look after his niece perfectly well, it would be pleasant for her and very useful for him. 'If she would stay with you for the next half hour,' he said,

'I'd be very grateful.' He fluffed the child's hair moved rapidly away. He saw Anthony and Gemma exchange worried looks, but they didn't actually object.

He strode over to join Rachel and the tall, emaciated, tweedy man he assumed was Barney Johnstone. 'Wonderful to meet you,' said the man in patrician accents. 'Time we made a start.' He led them over to the makeshift stage. Rachel shot Philip a nervous smile.

'I feel such a fraud, being here,' she whispered to him. 'No one has ever heard of me, why should I be part of the opening?'

Only a few weeks ago Philip might have resented having to share the limelight with someone else, but now he said, 'Probably more of them have heard of you than of me. Your rescue of the little Westie made quite a splash in the local paper.' He realised this was true and was pleased he had said it. Rachel pulled her pretty face into another grimace but they were climbing the steps to the stand now and there was no time for further discussion.

★ ★ ★

Anthony was beginning to get bored. He had never understood why people found horse-jumping the least bit interesting. He had tried to keep his views to himself as Gemma clearly thought otherwise, but now he was starting to resent the fact that not only was she fascinated by the spectacle, she also found the child they now had in tow much more appealing than she found him. He wasn't sure how long Gemma would be willing to remain in his company. Her father was busy in the cattle show ring just now, but that wouldn't last for ever.

'Do we really have to keep her with us,' he hissed, indicating the child with a nod of his head.

Gemma frowned. 'I think Mr Milligan's a bit busy just now, and she's a sweet little thing.'

'I wanted to walk around, see some of the stalls,' said Anthony mutinously. He had been amazed when Gemma agreed to spend some time at the show with him, but it wasn't working out as he hoped.

'Well, we can do that. Let's just see how the last horse does. If it gets less than eight faults it wins, but I doubt it'll manage, it's a hard course.'

'Mmm,' said Anthony, wondering how she knew it was a difficult course. Was she interested in horses? There was so much he didn't know about her.

'You can go off without us if you want, we'll catch up with you.'

'Oh, no, I'm quite happy to wait.' Anthony wasn't going to let her escape so easily.

The child at Gemma's side touched her hand shyly and said, 'Look, the chestnut horse is coming now. I hope it wins, I do hope it wins.' And the two of them were engrossed again, holding their breath at each twist and jump, groaning when the horse refused at the triple and applauding when it reached the finish with one second to spare.

'Right, can we get going now,' he said as soon as their celebrations had calmed down. He frowned at Amelia as she clung to Gemma's hand, swinging it gently. He wanted to be the one holding her hand.

Anthony's mood improved as they proceeded to wander around the large field where the stalls were set out in improvised avenues. Boroughbie Show wasn't a large one, not when compared with The Royal Highland Show in Edinburgh, or even the Dumfries and Lockerbie Show just south of here. But it was well attended and today the sun was shining brightly. Not being particularly interested in farm animals, and very keen to avoid Freddy Smith, he steered them towards the arts and craft section.

He came to a sudden halt before a stall displaying pictures of the bleak upland hills. They were stunning. 'Wow.' He looked more closely. These weren't paintings, he could see that much. Some were in black and white but others had colour shaded in, very faint, adding to the atmosphere of the high country. 'How are they done?' he asked. He was really impressed. His question had been addressed to Gemma but the man behind the stall answered him.

'They're prints. I'm a print maker.' He smiled brightly at them. He was a small, plump man with a fringe of dark hair all around his head, like a monk's.

'They're lovely,' said Gemma, but Anthony could tell she was just being polite. She wasn't awed by them as he was.

'How do you do them?' he asked, bending down to look more closely. He could see now that there were a few copies of each picture, and yet every one looked like an original.

'I work mostly in lino cut,' said the man. 'This is one, see? There's a lot of work in the design and the cutting of the stencils, like. Then you can print out up to fifty, depending on the materials. I don't tend to do more than that, I like them to still be special. They're right fine, are they no'?'

'I like the way you get the lines to . . . I don't know. But I like the way the lines are.' Anthony put his head on one side, examining the pictures more closely. 'I'd love to see how it's done.'

'Did you no' study Art at school? Sometimes they do stencilling there, that would give you the idea.'

'I wasn't allowed,' said Anthony, momentarily sulky. His parents, encouraged by Rachel, had thought academic subjects were more important.

'I've just done my Art Higher,' said Gemma. 'But we never did anything like this.'

The man took out one of his cards and handed it over. 'I'm Rupert Randall,' he said cheerily. 'My studio is on the Low Road going out of town towards Selkirk. I don't generally run an open studio, but if you're really interested why don't you drop by sometime?'

Anthony took the card and turned it around in his hand. This, too, had been hand printed. It was the pattern of an eagle repeated in a complicated circle. He'd love to know how you did that. 'That'd be cool,' he said. 'Thanks a lot.'

'That's very kind of you,' said Gemma politely.

Anthony would have liked to have stayed and talked some more but she ushered him away. 'Why'd you do that?' he said. 'I wanted to look through all this stuff, there was stacks of it we hadn't seen.'

'We were monopolising the whole stall. He's there to sell stuff not to talk to us, and we were keeping people away.'

Anthony hadn't noticed that, but maybe she was right. He stuck the card in the pocket of his jeans and said, 'Anyone for an ice cream? I think we deserve a break.'

* * *

Rachel found that she was actually enjoying her role at the Boroughbie

Show. She had never been prone to shyness, but had to admit to feeling a little intimidated before the formalities began. Once they were in the swing of things, however, she relaxed. Everyone was so friendly and appreciative, saying positive things for once about not only her rescue of Jinty but about Collington Kennels as well. She wished her parents could have been there to see it. Unfortunately her mother had been feeling a little under the weather and her father had insisted on staying home to keep her company.

Rachel had never shaken so many hands or smiled for so many photographs, but it was actually quite fun handing out the rosettes and medals. Everyone had worked so hard to get the best from their animals and it was lovely to see their efforts being rewarded. Freddy Smith came second in the Galloway Heifer Stirk section and even he managed a small smile of acknowledgement.

Of course, the bright sunshine helped

maintain the cheerful mood, as did the presence of Philip Milligan at her side. She had previously thought him rather reserved, but today the charm that was so apparent on the small screen was very much to the fore. He chatted with all and sundry, had his photograph taken time and time again, and still managed to make her feel special.

They had just presented the very last cup and Philip had touched her hand and said, 'I think we deserve a drink now, don't you?' when her mobile phone rang.

She smiled apologetically and withdrew to one side to answer it. As she did so she realised she had already missed two calls from home, unheard amongst all the noise.

'Hi, Mum,' she said. 'Sorry I missed you earlier . . .'

'It's Dad.'

Immediately Rachel felt panic. Her father never phoned her mobile unless it was absolutely unavoidable. 'What's happened? Where's Mum?'

'I wonder if you could come home, Rachel. Your mother's, er, rather unwell. I've called an ambulance and they should be here any minute. And if you could track down Anthony . . . ?' Her father's tone was as mild and polite as usual, but Rachel could detect the tremor in it.

'But what's happened? Tell me what happened.' Rachel was clinging to the small phone, desperate for information.

'You know your mother was feeling a little dizzy this morning? I persuaded her to have a lie down but when I took her up a cup of tea a little while ago I couldn't seem to wake her . . . '

'She's unconscious?' yelped Rachel. 'Is she . . . is she breathing?'

'Oh yes, dear, she's breathing. But she sounds horribly wheezy. They want to get her into hospital as soon as they can.'

'I'm on my way,' said Rachel. 'If the ambulance arrives before we do you go on to the hospital, we'll follow you.'

Her heart was beating so fast she

found it hard to concentrate. She looked desperately around for Anthony in the milling crowd and then realised that Philip was at her side.

'I can see there's a problem,' he said quietly. 'Can I help?'

'I need to get home. But I need to find Anthony first.' Rachel closed her eyes for a moment, to clear her head. She was supposed to be the organised one, she shouldn't be panicking.

'I said I'd meet Anthony and that very nice young lady in the tea tent, so that's most likely where they'll be. Why don't you head over there and I'll say our goodbyes here? I'll catch you up.'

'Thanks.' It was a relief to have someone take charge. Rachel jumped down the steps of the stand two at a time and set off across the emptying field. What was going on? How could her mother suddenly be so ill? She felt shaky with fear. It couldn't be anything serious, could it?

A Blossoming Friendship

Maggie Collington was taken to the Infirmary in Dumfries. Rachel and her father followed the ambulance in her car and Anthony stayed at home to look after the dogs, assisted by Philip Milligan and Amelia. Rachel couldn't quite understand how Philip had become so involved, but she didn't have the time or energy to object.

By the time they arrived at the hospital, Maggie had been taken straight to Intensive Care and all Rachel and her father could do was wait. The hospital canteen served surprisingly good coffee, but it was no comfort. Eventually, on their third visit to the ward, a white coated doctor came out to see them.

'How is she?' demanded Rachel and her father together.

'She's doing fine. We've stabilised her condition and are doing a number of tests, but our suspicion at the moment is that she has had a bad reaction to the new drug she has recently started. She may have been warned about dizziness and a rash?' He looked questioningly at his interlocutors.

Rachel shrugged and looked at her father. She felt horribly guilty. There had been so much to worry about recently, she hadn't given her mother's visit to the hospital outpatients the attention it deserved.

'She didn't say anything,' said her father with a sigh. 'But then Maggie does like to play down her own problems. She hates to feel a burden, not that she is of course. Why, look at me . . . ' He indicated the crutch that he still used to help him walk although the plaster had now been removed from his ankle.

'So if she stops taking the medication immediately she'll be all right?' asked Rachel.

'That is what we're hoping, but only time will tell.'

Rachel sat back in the hard chair and breathed properly for what seemed like the first time in hours. 'Thank goodness.'

'Can we go in and see her?' asked her father.

They were allowed to make a brief visit, to see for themselves that Maggie's breathing had improved. She couldn't talk to them as she was mildly sedated, but the nurse who showed them in assured them that they could phone for updates and they were welcome to visit again the next morning.

★　★　★

After the excitement of the Boroughbie Show and the anxiety of the hospital visit, Rachel was relieved when life settled into a calmer rhythm. Bookings in the kennels were picking up, although still lower than the previous year. Her mother had been transferred to a general ward and was due home any day. Her father could now walk short distances without a crutch. It was time, she decided, to turn her attention to Anthony.

'You've been really helpful around the kennels,' she said, catching up with him as he returned from walking three cairn terriers.

'Mmm.' Anthony gave each of the dogs a treat and let them back into their runs.

'Mum and Dad are paying you what they can, but things are a bit difficult at the moment as you know.'

'I know. I'm not complaining, am I?'

It was true that Anthony wasn't complaining, which was good, but nor was he making any decisions about what to do about his future. And that wasn't good.

'You'll need to confirm whether you're going to take up your place at university within the next two weeks,' said Rachel, perching herself on the garden wall. It might be easier to talk to him out here.

'So you and Dad keep saying.'

'So — have you decided?'

Anthony leant against the wall but looked at his feet, not at her. 'I don't know. I don't know if I want a career in computing any more.'

Rachel suppressed a sigh. It wouldn't help if she annoyed him even more than she usually seemed to do. She never intended to come across as the bossy elder sister but that was how he saw her.

'If you're not sure then you shouldn't do it. It's a four year course. That's a big commitment of time, not to mention money.'

Now Anthony did glance at her from beneath lashes so long they should have been a girl's. 'Are you serious? I thought you were all desperate for me to go.'

'Not if you don't want to. There's no point.'

'OK, then I won't go.' Anthony seemed genuinely relieved. 'The more I think about it the more I'm sure it's not what I want to do.'

Rachel was surprised and pleased to have got a decision out of him, but she wasn't going to leave it there.

'That's fine, if you're sure. We'll need to let the admissions people know. And then, if you're not going to do that, you'll need to think about what you are going to do.'

Now it was Anthony's time to sigh, a huge exhalation he didn't bother to try and hide. 'I don't know, do I? Everyone thinks you just know what you want to do, but I don't. Gemma's lucky, she's desperate to start her Business Studies course. I can't think of anything duller myself.'

Rachel thought Gemma was possibly as keen to get away from her difficult father as she was to progress her studies, but she didn't say so. 'It's good that you're getting on well with Gemma. She's a nice girl.'

'We're not going out,' said Anthony abruptly. 'She won't go out with me. Says her dad won't approve.'

'That's a shame,' said Rachel, thinking it would be a very good thing if Gemma left home. 'But you can still be friendly, that's something isn't it?'

'Hmm,' said Anthony and heaved himself away from the wall. He headed off down to the house, the conversation over. Rachel would have liked to discuss things further, and vowed to make the opportunity for a further chat in the next day or so.

She was about to follow him indoors when she spotted a piece of white paper on the ground. She bent down to pick it up and turned it over slowly in her hands. It was the card of an artist called Rupert Randall, based in Boroughbie. It was beautifully illustrated with black and white drawings of an eagle. Rachel remembered now how Anthony had raved about meeting this man, about how brilliant his work was. The man had apparently said that Anthony could call in at his studio, but he said he wasn't going to bother. He had said there was no point.

Rachel turned the card over in her hand again and wondered if she wouldn't pay a little visit herself.

★ ★ ★

Rachel found herself going out to lunch with Charlie McArthur. He had invited her out a few times recently, but for one reason or another she hadn't been able to go. This time she had accepted more because she felt bad for the earlier refusals than because she really wanted to go. Charlie was a nice enough guy but she suspected he had more interest in her than she did in him, and this made her uncomfortable.

'You look beautiful,' said her mother fondly when she went up to her bedroom to say goodbye. Maggie Collington had been discharged from hospital a few days earlier, but still needed to rest. At the moment she was agreeing to do so. 'Have a lovely time.'

'Thanks.' Rachel glanced down at her floaty pink and cream skirt which she had paired with a short maroon jacket. She hoped it wouldn't look like this was trying too hard.

'Charlie McArthur is a lovely man,' said her mother.

'I know.'

'He's got more than one or two of the local girls after him. It's very flattering that he's so keen on you.'

'Mum, we're just friends.'

Maggie nodded understandingly. Then she said, as though there was a connection, 'And have you seen anything of Philip Milligan recently?'

'No. No reason why we should. He was very helpful that night you were rushed to hospital, but he's got his own life, no doubt he's busy.'

* * *

Charlie took her to the Maybole House Hotel in a little village just outside Boroughbie. Rachel had forgotten what an attractive place it was, the four-storey house with its myriad of sash and case windows, flanked at right-angles on each side by two two-storey wings. In the square this created was a complicated knot-garden of herbs and flowers. 'It's very smart,' said Rachel, glad she had dressed up but worried now that Charlie was going to be spending rather a lot of money on her.

'The food's good, that's the main thing,' he said. That was one of the nice things about Charlie, he was so easy going it was hard not to relax when in his company. He wasn't moody and unpredictable, like someone else she could mention.

They were shown to their table. Charlie ignored the almost intimidating array of snowy-white cloths and polished silverware and chatted away about his work and the Boroughbie Show. Rachel found it was easy to join in, sipping the one glass of white wine she had accepted, and beginning to enjoy herself.

They had reached the pudding stage when there was a crash followed by the sound of two familiar voices in an unfamiliar altercation. Rachel's seat gave her a lovely view of the gardens, but she had her back to most of the room and had been unaware of who their fellow-diners were. Now she turned to see Philip Milligan and his little niece at a table not very far away, with a tumbler of some kind of coloured juice now spread over the white cloth and dripping on to the floor.

'You need to be more careful . . . '

'I'm sorry. I'm sorry.'

'Not a problem, sir,' said a waiter hurrying up with a pile of napkins and beginning the mop up operation.

'How many times have I told you?' said Philip to the girl. He was quite pink with embarrassment. This wasn't the sort of attention he was used to. The child looked close to tears.

Rachel moved to stand up, sure she could do something to help, and her action caught Philip's eye. 'Amelia . . . ' His voice tailed off.

'How nice to see you,' said Rachel cheerily, as though there hadn't just been a small disaster. She kissed them both on the cheek, taking herself by surprise. 'Are you here for lunch too?'

'This place was recommended,' said Philip stiffly. 'But I should have realised it really isn't suitable for a child.'

'They're very helpful,' said Rachel, impressed at the way the waiter had removed the plates, etcetera, whisked off the stained cloth and replaced it with another, all in the blink of an eye.

'I spilled my juice,' said Amelia, still looking horrified.

'These things happen,' said Rachel, patting her thin shoulder. Then she realised she had left Charlie alone at their table and with a few more words of encouragement, withdrew.

'That's that television guy, isn't it?' said Charlie. 'He did a good job at the show. Not surprising, of course, with you there to help him. How're his dogs doing?'

'They're fine,' said Rachel. 'Luckily.

You did a good job of sorting out Ben.'

'I heard Philip bought that lovely old house in the next valley to you. Is he going to settle in the area?'

'I presume that's the plan,' said Rachel, wishing they could talk about something else. To her relief, a waitress arrived to see if they wanted coffee, and Charlie was distracted.

When they left she made sure she didn't go too close to Philip's table, just raised a hand in a casual farewell. At Charlie's suggestion they took a walk in the hotel gardens, which fell away to the river at the back. She was about to suggest they head for home when she realised Philip and the child had joined them.

'Thank you for coming to my aid back there,' he said. She wasn't sure if he was being sarcastic. He hadn't needed her to jump in like that.

'No problem. Did you enjoy your meal?'

'Once we got over the accident, yes, it was fine.'

'I had a burger,' said Amelia. 'It was really big. I couldn't finish it.'

'It's a shame they don't do a children's menu,' said Philip.

'They serve generous portions, don't they?' agreed Charlie. 'I couldn't finish my steak, either, and I'm sure I've got a much bigger appetite than your niece.' He seemed quite taken with the child and took her down to the water's edge to see if they could spot any fish.

Philip hung back and Rachel felt she should stay with him out of politeness. He had been so good after the show, but now he was back to that supercilious tone she disliked so much.

He said abruptly, 'Amelia and I wondered if you'd like to come and have supper with us one day.'

Rachel was dumbfounded. She had expected, hoped even, that she might see some more of him after his helpfulness. He had phoned a number of times to ask after her mother, but he had never suggested meeting up. At first she had been too anxious to think anything of it, then she had told herself not to be silly. Why should Philip Milligan have time for someone like her?

And now this.

'Do I presume that is a No?' he said, his grim tone making her realise she hadn't yet answered.

'No . . . I mean, sorry, I was thinking. I'd love to come. That's very kind of you.' She met his eyes and felt herself beginning to blush. She looked quickly away. 'What day were you thinking of?'

'How about, say, Thursday? Yes?' His tone was cheerful now. 'If you come along late afternoon we can take the dogs for a walk and eat afterwards. Amelia would like that.'

Rachel immediately decided he was inviting her merely for Amelia's sake.

A Plan Backfires

Rachel hadn't forgotten she was going to do something about Anthony. On the Monday she made a trip into Borough-bie and sought out Rupert Randall's studio. She stood before the door for a moment, nervous now. She wasn't quite sure what she was going to say and had no idea if she would be welcome.

She tapped on the half-open door of what was clearly a converted garage, a square stone building with double doors.

'In you come,' shouted a voice, so friendly she felt herself relaxing.

The room she entered was large and airy, lit by numerous skylights. A small, balding man was bent over a worktable in the centre. 'I cannae stop the now,' he said. 'But take a seat, I'll no' be a minute.'

'Thanks. I'm sorry to disturb you.'

Rachel looked around for a chair, but found they were all being used to prop up canvases or hold piles of paper. She didn't mind. The place was fascinating enough for her just to stand and look. There were pictures everywhere, mostly the same distinctive black and white designs she recognised from the little card, but also sketches, water colours, and piles and piles of what she assumed to be artists' supplies — paper and ink and knives, brushes, sheets of lino and she didn't know what else.

She was amazed to see all this here, in a little back road out of Boroughbie. She had thought of this as an agricultural area, a little market town, and now realised there was so much more she didn't know about the place.

The man finished his task and wiped his hands on a cloth. 'Good afternoon to you,' he said with a twinkling smile. 'Now, what can I do for you?'

'I'm Rachel Collington. You won't know me, but I think you've met my brother.'

'I recognise you from the papers,' he said with a grin. 'You're the heroine.'

Rachel pulled a face. 'Hardly. My brother came up and spoke to you at the show, a tall fair-haired boy, nineteen-year-old?' She hoped the man remembered him. So much of her plan relied on that.

'Aye, I mind him. Had a young lady and a wee lassie with him, did he no'?'

'That's right. Our neighbour, Gemma, and the little girl was Amelia, niece of Philip Milligan who opened the show, but never mind about that. Anthony was really interested in your work.'

'He said so. I told him to come and see me.'

'Yes. The thing is, he's a bit . . . shy. And, I don't know, maybe it's just a teenage thing. He is really keen but he doesn't seem to know what to do with himself at the moment. He wanted to come but he wouldn't, so I thought I'd come and talk to you myself.'

'Aye?' said the man. His round face seemed amused by her interference and not necessarily pleased.

Rachel tried again. 'Anthony's not doing anything with himself at the moment. I wondered if he could spend some time with you as a, I don't know, an assistant or a dogsbody or whatever. He seems fascinated by what you do and if he could get a chance to see it close up maybe it would give him an idea . . . ' She tailed off. This had all made sense when she thought it through at home, but now, with the little man watching her silently from dark eyes she wondered if it wasn't an incredible intrusion. 'I'm sorry, it's probably a cheek to ask you . . . '

'He wants a job, does he?'

'He wouldn't expect you to pay him. He just needs to do something, you know? Something he's interested in, for once. He's been helping my parents with the kennels they run, but that's their interest, not his.'

'There's no much money in print-making,' said the man. 'It's not a great career.'

'I've not got as far as thinking of a career just yet,' said Rachel. 'First he needs to find out what he's interested in, then we can take it from there.'

The man continued to regard her in silence for a while. His cheery face did not lend itself to frowns, but he seemed to be considering. 'I'm busy enough at the moment, an extra pair of hands wouldnae go amiss.'

'That'd be brilliant.'

'I'm not anyone's nursemaid, mind. He'd have to think for himself.'

'Of course. He can do that.' Rachel hoped he could, at least.

'Tell him to come by and see me himself and we'll take it from there.'

'Thank you!' Rachel shook his hand enthusiastically.

* * *

Anthony was feeling very pleased with himself. He had taken the bus into Boroughbie with the vague idea of seeing Gemma. Apparently if he had

161

got up earlier he could have got a lift in with Rachel, but on the whole he was glad he hadn't. She would no doubt be wanting to give him some good advice about how to live his life and he was fed up of all that.

He had drifted in to the Boroughbie Arms. He knew Gemma didn't like him to interrupt her at work but he thought he'd have a little chat with Mrs Mackenzie, who was always so friendly, and find out when Gemma finished. And that was when Mrs Mackenzie had made her surprising suggestion.

'I suppose you're off to university yourself in a few weeks,' she had said, folding her arms across her ample chest and settling back for a chat.

'No, I'm not, actually.' Anthony had so far told hardly anyone this and still felt embarrassed.

'Did you no get a place?'

'Yes, yes I did. It's just I don't think it's what I want to do any more.'

'Aye, well. Sometimes it takes a while to decide what you want to do.' Mrs

Mackenzie was so understanding that Anthony thought perhaps he was doing the right thing. She continued. 'Be useful for the likes of me if a few more of you young people stayed around. I'm going to be short of staff when they all go off to college. It won't be so busy, of course, after the summer rush, but I'll still be a waiter-cum-barman short.' She smiled at him. 'I don't suppose you're looking for a job yourself?'

Anthony grinned back. A barman wasn't the height of his ambitions, but it would be a job, get him out of the house, earn some money. He would be independent at last. 'Actually, I think I am.'

They agreed on a trial period and a start date and Anthony took himself off to dissipate his excitement by a long walk around town until Gemma was free.

Gemma wasn't nearly as impressed by his news as he had expected and by the time he returned home his mood had taken a definite downward turn.

Gemma had also refused to go out with him again. He was starting to think her father was just an excuse. If she really liked him she would take the risk, wouldn't she?

Rachel greeted him with, 'You're late back. We were just about to start tea.'

Anthony shrugged. 'I'm not that hungry.'

'Come on through to the kitchen. Mum and Dad like it if we all eat together.'

Anthony sighed and followed her. He was actually quite hungry, but he was fed up of being bossed around by everyone.

'Had a good day?' said his mother. 'It's nice that you and Gemma are getting on so well.'

'Yeah.'

'I expect she'll be going off to college soon,' said his father, looking sadly across at Anthony. No-one had criticised him for his decision not to take up his place at Edinburgh University. They just looked unhappy, which was worse.

'Yes, she will.'

'Have you decided what you're going to do with yourself?' asked his mother, passing him the salad. 'Don't think I'm nagging, dear, but I just wondered.'

Rachel opened her mouth to say something but Anthony got in first. 'Actually, I got offered a job today.'

They all looked at him in amazement.

'That's great news,' said his mother.

'What is it?' said his father.

'It's barman at the Boroughbie Arms.' There was silence. 'I know it's not a great job, but it'll earn me some money. You're always telling me I should go out and get a job, aren't you?'

'You've had a whole year to think about these things,' said his father. 'We were hoping that now you would have a definite idea of what you wanted to do, no more of this drifting.'

'I thought you'd be pleased,' said Anthony.

'It's good that you've found something,' said his mother encouragingly.

'But it's not exactly got prospects, has it?' said Rachel. 'Are you sure it's what you want to do?'

'It's not for the rest of my life,' said Anthony. He felt like shouting, but his mother was already looking upset and he didn't want to make things worse. It was the first time she had ventured downstairs. 'It's just something to be going on with, until I find what I want to do.'

'I went to see Rupert Randall today,' said Rachel.

It was such an unexpected turn in the conversation that it took Anthony a moment to realise who she was referring to. 'You went to see Rupert Randall?'

'Ye-es.' For once Rachel looked slightly abashed. Their parents were just looking puzzled. 'I saw that card he gave you and I thought, well, I just popped in to have a look for myself. He does really amazing stuff, doesn't he?'

'Yeah. I said.'

'And I got talking to him and he just

happened to say that if you were interested in learning about what he does you could go and spend some time with him . . . '

The rush of fury was so strong and sudden that for the first time in his life Anthony understood the term seeing red. 'You what?' How dare Rachel interfere?

'I just thought . . . '

'I'm not a child.' He was really shouting this time. 'I don't need you to go arranging things for me. I can arrange things for myself. I've got myself a job in the hotel, haven't I? I don't need to go hanging around some loser artist.' What made it worse was this was exactly the thing he most wanted to do.

'Don't speak to your sister like that,' said his father. 'She's only trying to help.'

Anthony glared at them all. 'Can't you get into your head, I don't need any help?' He stood up suddenly, knocking his chair over. 'I wish you'd never come home.' He was pleased to see that Rachel looked quite aghast at the scene she had provoked. 'I'm not going anywhere near Rupert Randall, and you can tell him so.'

A Disaster Strikes

Maggie hated it when the family argued. She was very lucky, it didn't happen often. Rachel was a lovely girl, and Anthony seemed to be growing up at last, even though he and Rachel didn't always see eye to eye. He'd get over this latest tiff, she was sure. She didn't know why Rachel was so keen for her brother to visit this artist man, but if she thought it was a good idea no doubt it was.

Maggie sighed quietly. She felt rather stiff in the mornings these days. It was such a shame those new drugs had disagreed with her, they had reduced the aches in her joints so much she had hardly noticed them any more. Now the pain was as bad as it had ever been, especially first thing.

She was still feeling very tired, as well, but she hoped that was just the result of the anaemia they had picked up in the hospital. The staff had been so good to her at the Infirmary, she was really grateful to them, although she would be glad to see a little less of the place than she had over the last few months. At least John was back to full health now.

By the time Maggie had got herself up and dressed she was the only one at home. Anthony had gone off to the hotel, Rachel was doing the weekly food shopping and John was collecting a couple of Chihuahuas from their housebound owner. The owner was going into hospital for a little operation and the dogs were to come to the Collingtons. They had never had Chihuahuas in before and Maggie was looking forward to meeting them.

She strapped the new splints around her wrists. That nice young physiotherapist had said this might make movement easier for her, and she had been right. The heavier side of housework was still a struggle, but she could do most other things. Now Rachel was taking over some of her outdoor duties she was remembering how much she had used to enjoy herself in the kitchen, experimenting with new dishes. She decided to get out that wonderful new mixer John had bought her for Christmas and see what she might make today.

She was roused from the depths of a recipe book by a loud banging on the door.

Maggie hurried to open it, puzzled as to who it could be, and found Freddy Smith on the doorstep. He had a piece of string around the neck of a skinny black and tan dog, and an expression of fury on his face.

'Is this yours?' he demanded without preamble.

Maggie frowned down at the dog. The poor thing was shivering.

'No, I . . . '

He interrupted before she could say more. 'I don't see who else's it can be, if it isn't yours. We're not exactly close to the town here, are we? One of the reasons I moved here, less likelihood of idiots letting their dogs roam free on my land. Little did I know there'd be a business like yours on my doorstep.'

Maggie was taken back by his anger. They had tried to make friends with the man when he moved into the neighbouring farm a year or so after their own arrival, but he had always seemed to want to keep himself to himself. Gemma was a nice enough girl and Maggie liked to mother her when she got the chance, but if her father didn't want to be sociable the Collingtons were perfectly happy to respect his wishes.

She smiled her best smile. 'I'm afraid I really don't know this dog, but I'll take her off your hands if you want. Poor thing looks like she could do with a square meal, doesn't she? Then I'll contact the police and the Dog Rescue Centre and see if anyone knows where she's from.'

'You're saying she's not from here?'

demanded the man with a sneer on his dark face.

'We're a dog kennels, not a rescue centre,' said Maggie, puzzled.

'Ah, but I know you take strays too, don't tell me any different. I've heard all about you. What do your paying customers think about having their little darlings side by side with some flea-bitten mongrel?'

'We . . . ' Maggie wondered what on earth he was talking about. And then she recalled they had very occasionally taken a dog from the Rescue Centre in Dumfries. It only happened if the Centre was absolutely full, and if the Collingtons had a kennel free, and then only for a dog that had had a full health check and all its vaccinations. She wondered how Freddy Smith had heard about this. She hoped it wouldn't upset any of their clients.

She and John had thought long and hard before offering to do it, but they knew how Faye struggled to keep the Rescue Centre going and had wanted to help if they could. She said gently, 'That only happens very occasionally, and I can assure you that if we do have a dog here it wouldn't be allowed to run off. This one I've never seen before, but as I said I'll be happy to take her off your hands.'

Freddy's anger seemed to have abated somewhat and he looked slightly abashed. 'I was sure it would be yours. I met your daughter a while back, letting dogs run off their leads, so I know it happens. It's not good enough you know . . . '

Maggie held out her hand for the string. 'Thanks for bringing her down,' she said. 'I'm sorry you were inconvenienced. I'll take care of her now, shall I?' She hated unpleasantness and just wanted this conversation to be over.

'If you want,' said the man reluctantly. He let her take the make-shift leash and the dog began to faun around Maggie's legs. 'It better not happen again,' said the man as he turned to go. 'I'll have something to say if it does, so

I will.' Clearly he still wasn't convinced Maggie was telling the truth.

That, more than anything, annoyed her. But she bit her lip, called a polite goodbye, and withdrew into the house with the dog.

She walked carefully back to the kitchen. She had rushed to the door without her stick and the last thing she needed was to take a tumble. 'Well, my darling,' she said to the little dog who was still trying to ingratiate herself. 'How about a nice bowl of milk and biscuits? Then I'll see what we can do for you.'

She ran her hands over the dog's fur. Although it was thin, it appeared well cared for. There was no collar, but she wouldn't be surprised to find a family were desperately looking for the animal even now. Some dogs just were thin, and this one was certainly friendly. What a silly man Freddy Smith was, making such a fuss over nothing.

The weather, which had been so good for so long, took a sudden and decided turn for the worse. Heavy rain on the Wednesday night turned to a steady drizzle on Thursday. Rachel knew it was good for the land but it made cleaning, feeding and walking the dogs much more of a chore.

'We've been spoilt,' she said as she came in for lunch, her waterproof dripping.

'Hang that in the porch, please,' said her mother. 'I've already mopped the floor twice today.'

'You should let me or Anthony do the mopping . . .'

'Yes dear. But don't you think you do enough?'

'Dad's doing lots,' said Rachel quickly. She was worried he might be doing too much too soon on his weak ankle, but he enjoyed being out and about so much she didn't like to protest.

'You're still doing all the heavy work. Now come and sit down, I've made a nice broth to warm you up.'

'Lovely.' Rachel was delighted with

how well her mother had recovered from the scare she had given them all. It was lovely to see her pottering about in the kitchen again. 'Smells delicious. Dad'll be in shortly.' Rachel considered her mother, recognising the expression on her face. 'You're missing Una, aren't you?'

Una was the black and tan mongrel Freddy Smith had kindly deposited on them the previous day. Rachel suspected her mother had rather fallen in love with the animal, who certainly knew how to ingratiate herself. Unfortunately the dog's owners had been to collect her that morning and Maggie seemed to be missing the company. 'I'll bring one of the other dogs down for you, shall I?'

'I'm perfectly all right,' said Maggie, looking embarrassed. 'But she was a love, wasn't she? That poor young couple, they were so apologetic. They'd been walking her in the Netherton Forest and she'd slipped her lead and gone off after a deer. She was a rescue dog, did you hear that? They'd got her from Edinburgh. They'll make sure they tighten up her collar next time!'

'I'm sure they will. She was a nice wee thing.' Rachel had wondered fleetingly about adopting the dog herself, if the owner hadn't been found. But that wasn't to be. 'Where's Anthony?'

'He's gone into town. I said he could borrow my car. He seems to be enjoying his training sessions at the hotel.'

'Mmm.' The two women looked at each other and both decided to say no more. There wasn't a lot they could do to change Anthony's mind at the moment, and sometimes even Rachel realised it was better to let things lie.

'Did I tell you I'd be eating out tonight?' said Rachel casually.

'With that nice Mr Milligan. Yes, you did.' Her mother cheered up immediately. 'I'm glad you and he are getting friendly. Such a nice man.'

'That's what you say about everyone,' said Rachel.

'And it's usually true. What time will you be off?'

'I was supposed to be going late afternoon so we could take the dogs for a walk, but I can't see that being much fun in this weather.' Rachel frowned out of the window at the steadily falling rain. She had been looking forward to an excursion with Philip and Amelia and Bill and Ben.

'Perhaps it'll clear up,' said her mother, ever the optimist. 'And before I forget, I've been looking out the jam I made and there's a nice pot of blackcurrant you can take. Everybody likes a good homemade jam.'

'Especially yours,' said Rachel, secretly amused. She could tell that her mother was going to do everything she could to win over that nice Mr Milligan. He seemed to have supplanted Charlie McArthur in her plans for her daughter. Rachel hoped that Charlie had got the message on Sunday she just wanted to be friends. The next problem was convincing her mother she also just wanted to be friends with Philip. It would be easier if she could convince herself, first.

Her father appeared at that moment, carrying a little Yorkshire terrier wrapped in a towel. 'I thought Pixie might like to spend some time with you,' he said to his wife. Like Rachel, he must have noticed Maggie was missing her unexpected guest. He dried off the tiny creature and popped her down on the tiled floor. 'She gets a bit intimidated by those boxers in the run next to her.'

'Pixie's perfectly able to stand up for herself,' said Maggie Collington, indicating to the dog that she was welcome on her lap. The dog needed no second invitation. She leapt up, turned around three times and then settled down, her dark little eyes gleaming.

'How're you going to eat your lunch with her there?' said Rachel, unable to resist a smile.

'She'll go down in a minute. Isn't she a darling?'

John Collington washed his hands and came and sat down at the table. He frowned out of the window. 'I don't like this weather,' he said, taking a bowl of steaming broth from Rachel.

'Nor do I,' she said. 'Everything seems to take twice as long.'

'It's not just that it's inconvenient. I'm worried that so much rain falling after that long dry spell might cause us some problems. Have you seen how high the Inshie Burn is? It looks as though it might break its banks.'

'Surely it won't come to that,' said his wife. 'It's never happened before, and the rain is quite light now, isn't it?'

'But persistent. Ah, well, time will tell.'

Her father settled down to enjoy his food but something was niggling Rachel at the back of her mind. Why should the burn be close to flooding now if it had never done so before? Then she remembered something she had seen when she was walking Bill and Ben on the high hills all those weeks ago. Freddy Smith had had a digger up there, doing work on the watercourses.

181

Could that have something to do with it?

After lunch, however, the rain eased off and this worry was forgotten. She had more imminent concerns, such as what she should wear for a visit to Courockglen House. As the weather was improving, it looked like the proposed walk would be on. It would still be very wet underfoot, which suggested that trousers and sensible shoes were the best option.

Eventually Rachel decided on the compromise of three-quarter length trousers and a light jacket over the turquoise top in case it grew cold. She brushed her hair until it shone, applied a very little make up, and set off feeling more nervous than there was any reason to be.

Courockglen House looked as magnificent as ever in the late afternoon sun, with a dark sky behind. Rachel parked her car on the gravel at the front and by the time she had climbed out Amelia had already appeared at the front door, followed more slowly by her uncle.

'Hello, Miss Collington, we made you a pudding,' said the child, hopping from foot to foot. Her shyness seemed finally to have been forgotten.

'Call me Rachel,' said Rachel, bending to kiss the soft cheek. 'Miss Collington makes me feel like I'm your teacher. And what pudding have you made? You must know I love puddings.'

'It's a surprise,' said Philip, joining them at the bottom of the steps. He gave Rachel an even bigger surprise by bending to kiss her cheek. 'Lovely to see you,' he said, his voice so warm that she felt herself blushing.

'It's lovely to be here,' she said quickly, taking a step away. 'Isn't it lucky the weather has cleared up?'

'Yes.' Philip seemed to be having problems taking his eyes off her.

'Uncle Philip says it might rain again soon,' piped up Amelia. 'So if we're going to go for a walk we should go now.'

'Excellent idea,' said Rachel, relieved at the distraction. 'I'll just get out the jam my mother has sent for you and then I'm ready to go.'

They walked up through the trees behind the house, a route Rachel had never followed before. The steady drip from the leaves was a constant accompaniment, but the path they walked on was a bridleway, wide enough to avoid their getting too wet themselves.

Amelia cavorted ahead with the two dogs and the adults watched them fondly.

'She seems to be coming out of her shell,' said Rachel.

'Yes. She's not really a bad kid.'

Rachel glanced sideways at him and realised from his smile that he was attempting a joke. 'You're enjoying having her to stay,' she said.

He nodded. 'I didn't expect to, but I am. It's playing havoc with my writing schedule, but if I get up early I can get a little done each day. And I have to admit, she's rather good company.'

'That's great,' said Rachel approvingly. She had never had difficulty getting on with young children herself, but she knew many childless adults did. 'She tells me you took her to Edinburgh Zoo last week, that was good of you.'

'We both enjoyed ourselves. I'll be quite sad when she has to go back.'

'When will that be?'

'My sister isn't recovering as quickly as she had hoped, but she thinks she'll be home in about a fortnight.'

'She must be missing her daughter. And no doubt Amelia is missing her parents, although she certainly seems happy enough.'

'They talk quite often on the phone. It's costing me a fortune.' But Philip smiled again as he said this, showing he really didn't mind. Rachel was amazed at how much he had mellowed. 'Bill and Ben will miss her even more than I will when she goes back. We're planning for her to come and stay again next summer.'

'It sounds lovely. I'm so glad the visit

has worked out well.'

'Not nearly as much as I am,' said Philip, with a touch of his old ironic tone.

They reached the brow of the hill, above the tree line now, and paused to take in the views on all sides. The dark clouds were more threatening than ever and they decided to turn for home.

'How are things with you?' said Philip. 'Are you pleased with your move to Scotland?'

'Yes, I'm loving it. The dogs are a joy to work with and I'm really enjoying seeing more of my parents. I didn't realise how much I worried about them, being so far away.'

'How's your mum?'

'Much better, thanks. The only problem is, the drug she had such a nasty reaction to was actually making her arthritis much better. Now she's had to stop taking it she's in quite a bit of pain. Not that she complains, of course.'

'Your parents are lucky to have you

around to help.'

'No,' said Rachel firmly. 'I'm lucky they're willing to let me stay with them. It's wonderful up here.' She gestured around at the vast green hills that could still be seen beyond the trees.

'Not bad, is it?' agreed Philip. Then, as heavy drops began to fall from the darkened sky, he called to Amelia to run the last little way, and took Rachel's hand to hurry her along. Rachel liked the feel of his warm strong hand around hers. She wished she knew how he felt in return.

★   ★   ★

Rachel arrived home from the meal at Philip's house in an excellent mood. They had got along surprisingly well. She hadn't stayed too late. She didn't want to impose. She reached home soon after nine. Her mother was already in bed and her father was watching television.

'It's raining again,' she said unnecessarily. The downpour could be heard pounding on the roof of the conservatory.

'I know.' Her father frowned. 'I'll just watch the end of Michael Palin and then I'll go out and do the last check on the dogs. I want to have another look at the burn, too.'

'I can do that,' said Rachel.

'Why don't you make us a cup of tea, then we can do it together?' He turned back to his programme and Rachel went to do as he asked. She noted that her mother had been making dropped scones and put some of these on a plate for him.

She was glad of the warmth of the hot drink when they did finally venture outside. It might only be late August but the wind had risen and the temperature felt more like late autumn. She huddled inside her waterproof, glad of the brief shelter as she popped inside each of the kennels to check on the dogs.

Her father had brought a heavy torch with which he lit the path towards the burn. Away from the electric lighting of the yard it was already very dark, making it feel more than ever like autumn.

'I don't like the sound of that,' he said, raising his voice to be heard above the roar of the water.

Rachel knew what he meant. The water was coming down in a howling torrent, almost at the top of the banks and, in one or two places, already over it. She had to force herself to take the last couple of steps to have a proper look. The swirl of the water in the flickering light was frightening.

'What'll happen if it bursts its banks?' she shouted, putting a hand on her father's arm to steady her.

'It'll come right through the yard,' he replied grimly. 'Look, it's already starting. You see that stream there? That wasn't there an hour ago. It must be already breaking down the banking further up.'

'But if it goes through the yard it'll flood the house,' said Rachel in horror.

'Not only that, it'll flood the west end of the kennel block. I think we need to move the dogs. In fact, I think we need to move ourselves, fast. Look out, it's coming over.'

Her father's dodgy ankle forgotten, they turned tail and ran.

The water that followed them was not a great wave, rather a steady, dirty flow that picked up speed gradually. Once they were back in the yard Rachel and her father cut back behind the higher kennels for shelter, and took stock. The water by-passed them here, but her father was right, it was already seeping into the lower kennels on the west side and lapping around the back door of the house.

'Dogs first,' he said as they took all this in. 'There are two kennels empty on this side, just grab everything and move them over, the cairns into the big one, the boxers in the other. I don't know about the Yorkie . . . '

'She can come in the house, safer there. I'll grab her and take her in. Then

I'll start moving things upstairs. That's the only thing we can do, I can't see any way we can stop the water coming in.'

'You're right. Give Pixie to your mother and let her know what's happening. But whatever you do don't let her come out in this.'

The water was getting deeper by the minute, swirling across half the yard now before racing towards the house. Some had already found a track for itself down the easterly side of the building and away, but with each passing minute the waves lapping at the kitchen and conservatory doors grew higher.

Rachel pushed her way into the end kennel and swooped down to rescue the tiny Yorkshire terrier, who was standing quivering on her sleeping shelf. She seized the bedding with her, but there was no time for more. The water was almost at the top of her Wellington boots and made her stagger with the force of the flow as she recrossed the yard to the house. One glance told her opening the back door would bring the flood straight inside so she struggled around to the front.

Here the porch light showed her the surreal sight of Anthony climbing out of the car on to the perfectly dry gravel, whilst two yards behind him the torrent flowed round the house and shot across the road.

'What's going on?' he said, pushing his damp blond fringe from his eyes.

'Inshie Burn's flooded. Can you go and help Dad move the dogs? I'm taking Pixie in the house and then I'll see what I can use to sandbag the back doors. Not that they'll hold the water for long. You and Dad will need to come in round the front.'

'I can't believe it,' said Anthony, unable to take his eyes off the flying water.

'Just go, OK?' shouted Rachel. 'There's no time to waste. And for goodness' sake keep an eye on Dad, if he should fall again . . . '

'I'm on my way,' said Anthony.

This time he did move, disappearing at a run around the side of the building, paying no attention to the water pouring over the smart shoes he had worn for an evening at work.

Rachel took Pixie upstairs where she found her mother already struggling into her dressing gown. 'What's happening?' Her mother's breathing was heavy again with anxiety.

'The burn's, er, a bit high,' said Rachel, trying to be soothing. 'We need to move some of the dogs. Can you keep Pixie here?'

'I'll come down and help. It's going to come into the house, isn't it? We need to move things.'

Rachel thought of how little strength her mother had in reserve for lifting and carrying, walking up and down the stairs. Yet she knew her mother was incapable of sitting and doing nothing in a crisis.

'You stay here and I'll pass things up to you,' she said.

And so the next hour was spent

ferrying anything Rachel felt could be rescued from the kitchen and conservatory where the water was flooding in. John and Anthony soon appeared to help and most of the furniture was saved. The carpets, however, were ruined, and the fridge and cooker, far too heavy to be lifted quickly, were almost certainly finished. The water was almost up to knee height at one point, before it began to subside as rapidly as it had risen.

Midnight found the four of them sitting slumped in Maggie and John's room, wet and breathless and totally exhausted. The only light they had was candles, the electricity having failed long since.

'I've checked all the dogs again, they're fine,' said Anthony.

'Pixie's certainly very happy,' said Rachel, cuddling the tiny dog to her. Now the activity was over shock was setting in and she was beginning to shiver.

'Nothing else we can do tonight, so I

suggest we all try and get some sleep,' said her father.

'What if the water rises again?' said his wife.

'I don't think it will,' said Anthony. 'Believe it or not, the sky's clear now. Not a cloud in sight. The worst is over.' Of all of them, he seemed to have come out of the ordeal the best. His slim young face was wreathed in smiles. 'Wow, that was quite something, wasn't it? Good job no one and no dog was hurt.'

'But think of what it'll take to clean up,' said Rachel, put out by his cheerfulness. 'Three rooms downstairs are wrecked, plus half the kennels. The electricity's out and we daren't trust the water supply.'

'It'll all look better in the morning,' said her mother, patting her arm gently. 'You get yourself off to bed. Put an extra blanket on, you want to make sure you keep warm. Shall I get it for you?'

'No, no,' said Rachel, realising that she was being pathetic. 'Don't worry about me, I'll manage.' She took Pixie away with her, to use as a living hot water bottle. Even so, it took a long time before she was warm and calm enough to sleep.

Anthony Proves His Worth

Philip decided to call in on the Collingtons the day after Rachel had come for a meal. He had enjoyed her company even more than he had anticipated and had only been sad that she had left so early. Now he remembered her father's open invitation to drop in and decided that this was a good time to take him up on it. Usually he was reticent about calling on people unannounced, but his desire to see Rachel outweighed any worries. Amelia also thought this an excellent idea and they set off soon after breakfast.

He was stunned to find the house in chaos, water lying in puddles in the downstairs rooms and the whole family looking rather the worse for wear.

'Goodness, what has happened?'

It was John Collington who explained about the flash flood from the stream that normally ran behind and beside the property. 'No real harm done,' he concluded heartily. 'No damage to life or limb at least.'

'Sorry we can't offer you tea or coffee,' said Rachel, pushing hair from her eyes with a tired gesture. 'We're still without power and we need electricity to pump the oil to the Aga so even that isn't working,'

'You should have phoned, you could all have come and stayed at Courock-glen,' exclaimed Philip, surprising even himself with his generosity.

'We couldn't leave the dogs,' said Rachel quickly.

'We have an electrician arriving any time now,' said her father. 'We'll be fine. I've managed to persuade Maggie to stay in bed, it's the warmest place for her. Rachel and Anthony and I will soon have this place shipshape.'

'Actually, I've got to go to work in

half-an-hour,' said Anthony. He seemed the least perturbed by all the upset. 'I suppose I could phone the hotel and see if they can manage without me, but I don't want to let them down so soon after I've started. And I did say I'd give Gemma a lift.'

'You go, we'll be fine,' said his father.

Rachel sighed. For the first time since Philip had met her she seemed vulnerable, and the sight of her pale, strained face did something very strange to his heart. 'You certainly will,' he said firmly. 'Because Amelia and I are going to help, aren't we Melie? The first thing I'm going to do is go back home and make some flasks of coffee. Once you've had that you'll all feel much better.'

'You don't need to . . . ' said Rachel doubtfully.

'Very much appreciate the offer,' said her father, smiling now.

Philip nodded his agreement and departed.

Philip had forgotten how much fun

sheer physical hard work could be. He had paid people to clean and redecorate Courockglen House, thinking that he didn't have time for such things himself. Now he wondered if he wouldn't have felt closer to the place if he had put in a little more effort.

The first part of the day was spent sweeping out the awful mud that covered all of the ground floor. Then he and Rachel began to pull up the ruined carpets whilst John turned his attention to the kennels. These were his priority. Fortunately they had been less affected and by the nature of their design were easier to put to rights. He took Amelia with him to 'keep the dogs amused', something which she delighted in.

'You really don't need to put yourself out like this,' said Rachel when they took a rest after heaving the living room carpet outside. 'It's very kind of you but we don't want to be a nuisance.'

'You're not a nuisance,' said Philip. 'Isn't this what neighbours are for?'

True enough, a number of nearish

neighbours had come by to see how they were faring, one had arranged a skip and another brought sandwiches. Only Freddy Smith had made no contact. The Collingtons, in their good-natured way, had worried if he too had had problems. Anthony had offered to go and find out and had reported that the farmhouse was unscathed and the farmer not very pleased to see him, although Gemma had been happy to take her lift into town.

'You're not really a neighbour,' said Rachel with a faint smile.

'I'm a neighbour and a friend,' he said firmly and was rewarded by a brighter smile this time.

It was all going so well, and then Philip began to have his doubts. Rachel was looking pale and wan, but she refused to lean on him. Her attitude brought back all his old doubts. Perhaps he was better off on his own, taking the little successes he could manage, not putting his heart at risk.

Letting in affection for Amelia had made him think he could open himself up to other things, too. Now he wasn't so sure.

The final straw was when Charlie McArthur called round on the Sunday, ostensibly to check on the dogs who had been in the kennels during the floods.

'They're absolutely fine, you did exactly the right thing,' he said approvingly to the Collingtons, having done his round.

'Thank goodness for that,' said John. 'We did our best, but you're never sure, are you? And most people have been very understanding, but one or two we couldn't get hold of on the phone so I just hope they haven't been worrying.'

'Most people trust you implicitly to look after their dogs,' said Rachel. 'After all, there has only been one owner with anything to complain about since the kennels opened.' She glanced meaningfully at Philip and he felt hurt. It had been worrying for him when Ben had been injured. He didn't feel he had overreacted but he suspected she did.

'It's so good of you to come out,' she said, smiling now at Charlie. She seemed perfectly happy to accept help from him.

'I wanted to see how you were,' said the vet, smiling warmly back. That was enough for Philip. He wasn't going to make a fool of himself. He and Amelia left very soon after.

★　★　★

'I've got an idea,' said Anthony. It was ten days or so since the flood and things were slowly getting back to a sort of normality.

He and Rachel were unloading sacks of dog food from the car and he had paused at the door of the store room.

'What kind of idea?' asked Rachel.

'Come in here for a minute and I'll tell you.' He had lowered his voice to a whisper and waited till she was inside the tiny room before he spoke again.

'You know it's Dad's sixtieth birthday soon?'

'Yes, in three weeks' time.'

'Well, I thought, why don't we have a party for him? Things have been a bit grim recently and I thought a party would really cheer us all up.'

Rachel stared at her brother in amazement. 'That's a really good idea.'

'You don't need to sound so surprised,' said Anthony.

'Well, I am. What on earth made you think of it?'

'Actually, it was something that happened at work. The main restaurant was taken over for a sixtieth birthday party last night. It had been arranged as a secret and you could tell the guy they had done it for was really chuffed. It made me think.'

'It's an excellent idea,' said Rachel, grinning broadly. 'I wonder if we should do it as a surprise or not? We'll have to ask Mum and see what she thinks. It'll be fun. You're a genius. I'll tell her you thought of it.'

'As long as you do all the organising,' said Anthony quickly, showing that he hadn't changed all that much.

'Of course. You don't need to worry about that. I suppose we had better go back outside or Dad is going to wonder what on earth has happened to us.'

As they made their way back across the yard, which still looked rather bare from the scouring water, Anthony cleared his throat and said, 'By the way.'

'Mmm?'

'I went round to see Rupert Randall yesterday.'

Rachel swung round to stare at him. 'You did? But I thought you were dead against it. I even phoned and explained to him I'd got the wrong end of the stick . . . '

'You hadn't, really,' said Anthony apologetically. 'I just felt you were interfering.'

'I suppose I was.'

'Well, anyway,' said Anthony, shrugging off that topic. 'I thought I'd go and see him. He's a really genuine guy. And it doesn't seem impossible for me to spend some time with him and still do this hotel job. I'm going to go round on Monday and we'll see.'

★   ★   ★

Rachel waited for a chance to discuss Anthony's idea of a birthday party with her mother, but every time she was in the house her father seemed to be there too. The insurance company's assessors had been to view the flood damage and now they were in the 'drying out' stage before they could think of putting everything back to rights. Her father was doing what he could to make the kitchen usable, meantime.

'It could have been worse,' said her mother, one of her favourite expressions. They had paused for a cup of tea mid-afternoon. 'Your father's idea of using the flagstones in here and the hall and conservatory has meant these floors are virtually unscathed.'

'Pity about the skirtings and the

lower parts of the wall,' said Rachel.

'But with the Aga being set on it's plinth, that too has come through very well,' said her mother. 'And now the electricity is back on I'm going to get a replacement fridge. We'll be able to function very nicely. I'm sorry you've had to put up with all this,' said her mother. 'Not at all what you expected when you came back home.'

'I don't mind for me,' protested Rachel quickly. 'It's just such a shame, after all your hard work.'

'These things happen,' said her father. 'We were just unlucky. Highest August rainfall in a century, or so they say. And all in the last week.'

Rachel suddenly recalled the digger she had seen high up on Freddy Smith's land. She couldn't help wondering if any work he had done there had added to their problems. She didn't like to mention it to her parents.

'Philip hasn't been round for a few days,' said her mother, watching Rachel's face. 'He was a great help at the beginning. I hope he doesn't think we were taking advantage, using his house for showers and so on.'

'He offered,' said Rachel, but she too was wondering what had caused this silence. They had seemed to be getting on so well. Maybe he was just moody. If so, they were better off without him. She was sure that was the right opinion. She just wished she didn't think about him quite so much.

'Wonderful place he's got there,' said her father. 'I bet it has got a fascinating history of its own.' He grinned. He had clearly enjoyed the chats he had had with Philip, who had seemed to prefer his company to anyone else in the family. 'If he can't find out, no one can. Quite an impressive young man.'

'You haven't heard anything from him?' Maggie asked her daughter.

'No, I haven't.' Then Rachel realised she might have been a little abrupt. 'No reason why I should have, of course. He's probably busy catching up with work on his book, after spending all that time here.'

Her mother nodded in a way that made Rachel worry. She was quite pleased when her father went out to walk some dogs and she could change the subject to the possible birthday party. Her mother thought the idea was brilliant and Rachel made sure they kept the conversation on that for the rest of the afternoon.

★ ★ ★

'Are we going to go and see Rachel today?' asked Amelia. She had been asking the same question for days.

Philip sighed. He would love to go and see Rachel, too, but he didn't know whether she would be pleased to see them. She had been punctilious about thanking him for all his help after the flood, but her gratitude towards Charlie McArthur had been far warmer.

'I want to go and see Rachel,' said Amelia again.

'Maybe we'll go over later on, see how they're doing.' Philip wanted to go too, if he could have been sure of his reception.

'I'd like that.'

'But this morning we're going to go shopping. Remember we were going to choose something for you to take back as a present for your mother?'

'Yes.' Amelia gave a little skip of pleasure. She was a different child from the one who had arrived all those weeks ago.

They went to Moffat rather than Boroughbie. It was a touristy town with plenty of gift shops for Amelia to browse in. It also meant a drive past Collington Kennels, so provided the ideal excuse for dropping in on their way home.

Philip was starting to get used to the local way of doing things. The slower pace of life, the way you had to have a little chat in every shop. Even in the massive Woollen Mill centre, which specialised in Scottish knitwear, the staff were happy to stop and talk.

'Terrible weather it's been, hasn't it?' said one little round woman, it was quite a common opening gambit. 'Are you here on holiday? I hope you've seen some sunshine.'

'I'm on holiday,' said Amelia, her voice still soft but no longer so shy. 'I'm going home soon and I'm going to buy a present for my mummy.'

'Your daughter?' said the woman to Philip, smiling fondly at the child. He had to admit she was a pretty little thing.

'Niece,' he said. 'She's been staying for the school holidays. The weather's been mixed, it started off lovely but the last couple of weeks haven't been so good.'

A middle-aged couple nearby joined in the conversation. 'It's been wet here, has it? We've just got back from the Canaries and we didn't see a drop of rain the whole fortnight.'

'Very wet,' said the shop assistant. 'I hear there were even floods over

Boroughbie way.'

'That's right,' said Philip, pleased for once to have some bit of local knowledge. 'The Collington Boarding Kennels had a bad time of it, water from the burn behind them flooded right through the place.'

'Collington Kennels?' asked the wife of the couple, looking horrified.

'Yes, the ones on the road between here and Boroughbie. The family managed very well, considering.'

'They said the water was up to here,' said Amelia, wide-eyed, showing a height almost at her thigh.

'Well maybe not quite that deep,' said Philip quickly, wondering why the couple looked so concerned. 'Anyway, young lady, have you made a decision yet? The cashmere scarf or the brooch, what's it to be?'

The shop assistant reluctantly turned from the fascinating topic of the weather to helping the child with her purchases.

★　★　★

When Philip and Amelia returned to the car park they found a crowd of people around one of the cars. As they neared, Philip realised with a sinking heart it was his Freelander. He was rather proud of this vehicle, the first he had ever purchased new, and he hurried over.

'What's happened?' he demanded. A solidly-built, dark-haired man, a couple of teenagers and what looked like half a coach-party turned as he approached.

'This your car?' said the man.

'Yes, it is. I . . . ' Then Philip saw the damage. Someone had driven into the rear off side. Even with the hefty bumper of the Freelander, the damage was severe. All the lights were broken and the bodywork buckled. 'Who did this? What on earth's happened?'

'It wasnae us,' said one of the youths quickly.

'It was a white pickup,' said the dark-haired man. 'Luckily I was just getting out of my own car and saw the whole thing. I shouted at him to stop but he ignored me. He was reversing too fast out of that space there, see. He must have known he'd hit something but he just drove off.'

Philip could feel himself shaking with anger. 'This is going to cost a fortune, not to mention the inconvenience. And I suppose I'll have to claim against my own insurance if we don't know who did it.'

'Ah, but we do,' said the dark-haired man. 'I took a note of his number. I don't like to see people getting away with something like that.' He handed over a scrap of paper on which he had scribbled the registration number.

'Quick thinking, son,' said someone. 'Well done.'

'You'll probably need to get the police involved,' advised another of the coach party. 'Report it to them, they can trace the van for you.'

The coach party began to drift away and Philip used his mobile to call the police. Then he took down the names of the two youths and the very helpful dark-haired man. He was an outdoor type who identified himself as, 'Freddy Smith, Inshie Heights Farm.' The name rang a bell with Philip, but he didn't have time to think about that now.

'You've been really helpful,' he said, shaking the man's hand. 'I can't thank you enough. If you hadn't taken down the number that driver would have got away with it.'

'Don't like to see people breaking the law,' said the man in the same abrupt tones. 'Too many people try it on, littering, building without permission, I don't know what. It's our responsibility to see these things don't happen.'

It was a good hour later when he and Amelia finally left the town. By this time Philip's patience had well and truly run out. He hated bureaucracy and was still smarting from the damage to his beautiful car. He supposed he should be relieved it was still driveable.

'Are we going to go and see Rachel?' asked Amelia as they approached the Collington's white cottage.

'Not today,' said Philip. He wasn't in the mood for being sociable. He had also just remembered where he had heard the name Freddy Smith before. He was the Collington's neighbour, who Rachel claimed was thoroughly unpleasant. Philip hadn't found him unpleasant at all, which only increased his doubts about Rachel. He really didn't understand her.

You'll Make A New Life Up There

To Anthony's surprise, life seemed to be going OK at the moment. The whole of the last year, which had supposed to be his fun 'gap' year, he had been dogged by doubts about his proposed university course. Now he had made the decision not to pursue computing studies he felt free. Rachel was right, if he didn't want to follow that career then there was absolutely no point in doing the course.

At first he had resented Rachel's presence at home, but he was starting to realise she wasn't all bad. And also, oddly, that she wasn't as capable as he had always assumed her to be. She had been really thrown by the flood, more so than their father, who had concentrated on working to solve the problem, or their mother, who had taken her lead from her husband and vowed not to worry.

Rachel seemed to think there was something they could have done to avoid the catastrophe, and the water had frightened her more than he would have expected. Funny to think that tough old Rachel could be frightened.

The only down side to life was that Gemma would soon be going away to Glasgow. She had still refused to 'go out' with him, but she seemed to enjoy his company. With both of them working at the hotel he saw almost as much of her as even he desired. Maybe once she was no longer living at home she would give him a chance? Or maybe she would meet a student as bright and hardworking as herself, with a good career in prospect, and forget all about him? The thought was horrifying.

He wished she wasn't quite so excited about the adventure ahead of her.

'I'm going to miss you,' he said

gloomily as she chatted away about her room in the Halls of Residence.

'You can come and visit. And I'll come home to see Dad as much as I can, he'll be lonely without me.'

Secretly Anthony thought she would be mad to come and spend time with her father who made life so difficult for her now. 'You'll make a new life up there, you'll forget all about us.'

'Rubbish,' she said, laughing. 'You see your friend, James, and others who are away at college, don't you? I thought you were out with them last night.'

'I was. But that was only because you wouldn't go out with me.'

'I had to cook Dad's meal, you know that. Anyway, time to go back in, that's our coffee break over.'

They had been sitting on a bench in the back garden of the hotel, glad of a few minutes fresh air. Anthony had been delighted that Mrs Mackenzie seemed to be scheduling their breaks to coincide.

And then, the very next day, he managed to upset Mrs Mackenzie.

He didn't mean to. That was the last thing he would have wanted, she had been really cool with him, first of all offering him the job and then not making a big fuss when he made the odd mistake.

The evening started well enough. It was a Friday and therefore rather busy with a mixture of locals and hotel residents. James and a couple of Anthony's other friends came in for their first drink of the evening. This wasn't their normal drinking haunt, but they said they wanted to see how he was getting on. It was a bit embarrassing, having to pull their pints, with them joking he wouldn't get the head right, but he managed OK. Then Stewart, the older barman, gave them a look, and they took their drinks off to a table and left him in peace.

'You getting on all right?' asked Stewart.

'Mmm.' Anthony nodded, unsure if the man was annoyed at the noise his friends had been making. Most of the clientele were middle-aged and frowned at the continuing hoots of laughter from the boys. Anthony wished James hadn't brought Russell Simpson with him, he was always far too loud.

'You're doing fine. Can you get some more bottles of dry white from the cellar? We've nearly run out. I'll deal with this lot.'

Anthony did as he was bidden, pleased to have got off lightly. When he returned Stewart was serving a grey-haired man who looked vaguely familiar.

'So I said to my wife, I said, if they can't look after wee Pixie the way we do at home she's no going back there.'

Anthony's ears perked up. He recognised the name of the little Yorkshire terrier immediately and recalled now that she was owned by an elderly couple from Boroughbie. What on earth was the man talking about?

'They're aye in the papers one way or another, those kennels. Makes you think, doesn't it?' The man took a satisfied swallow of his pint and wiped the froth from his upper lip.

Anthony stepped forwards. 'And which kennels would that be you're talking about?'

'Now, now,' said Stewart, frowning at his tone.

'Collington Kennels, they call them. Always seemed all right before but with all the troubles we had with our flight back and then coming home to find Pixie in a fair state, my wife's up to high doe.'

'What's wrong with Pixie?' demanded Anthony.

'Nothing wrong, as such. But they had a massive flood out at the place. Know it, do you? Out on the Moffat Road. Not that they told us about the flood, oh no. Pixie could have been washed away for all we'd have known about it if I hadn't heard it mentioned in the town.'

'That's my parents' kennels you're talking about,' said Anthony, feeling the anger rising. 'If you have anything to complain about you should speak to them directly.'

'Anthony, there are customers waiting,' said Stewart.

'If your parents can't be bothered to speak to me about what Pixie had to go through I don't see why I should go asking them anything. But you can tell them from me, my Yorkie won't be going back there, not after the way she was treated.'

Anthony couldn't believe anyone could be so unreasonable. And about his parents, who would never harm anyone. 'Don't be so ridiculous! You don't know how she was treated. I do 'cos I was there and I can tell you she was safe and sound in the house the whole time. Not a single dog was harmed in any way, but with Pixie being so small she was the first one we took inside. My mother had her on her lap and the dog loved every minute of it.' He glowered at the man. 'Maybe that's why my parents didn't say anything, because there was nothing to say!'

'Well now young man . . . ' began Pixie's owner, put out by the reaction he had provoked and going rather red in the face. 'That's as maybe, but how was I to know? They were talking about a river running through the place and I don't know what.'

'You shouldn't believe everything you hear,' continued Anthony, and then found himself being pulled sharply away by none other than Mrs Mackenzie herself.

'I need a hand in the back kitchen,' she said loudly.

It was only then Anthony looked around and realised every conversation in the bar had stopped. They were all staring at him. Not the sort of scene Mrs Mackenzie wanted played out in her lounge bar on a busy Friday night.

* * *

'I can't believe you got into an argument like that,' said Rachel, not for the first time.

'I was upset. The man was being so nasty and it wasn't fair.'

'But there are ways of dealing with these things.' Rachel glanced through to the conservatory where her parents were watching television. Anthony had been right to tell them of the incident at the Boroughbie Arms Hotel, but she feared that it had upset her parents more than they were saying.

Physical problems such as the flood did not seem to trouble them nearly as much as people speaking badly about the kennels. Her father had tried to phone Mr Donaldson, Pixie's owner, to put things straight, but all he had got was an answer phone. He had left a message but the Donaldsons hadn't phoned back.

'It's so unfair,' said Anthony, his young face unusually grim. 'I wonder who has been saying bad things about us?'

'Who knows?' Rachel shook her head. It was horrible to think that someone had it in for them. 'Anyway, shouldn't you be off to work?'

'I'm not working tonight. I wasn't rostered to work before all this happened, but now I don't know if Mrs Mackenzie will want me back. She was pretty upset.'

'Not surprising,' said Rachel, and then relented, seeing how troubled her brother looked. 'Look, if she didn't tell you not to come back I'm sure she'll be OK. Probably a good thing you're not working today, give her time to get over it.'

'I suppose,' said Anthony, still gloomy.

'So are you going out with James? Or Gemma?'

'Don't feel like it. I think I'll just have an early night. I'm taking Gemma's place serving breakfasts tomorrow so I'll have to be up first thing.'

'Good for you,' said Rachel encouragingly. She was amazed at how conscientious he was about his hotel work. 'And you've got Monday to look forward to, with Rupert Randall.'

'If I don't mess that up too,' said

Anthony, but his expression wasn't as gloomy as his words.

*   *   *

Rachel and her mother were busy planning the sixtieth birthday party. Her mother had taken to the idea with alacrity and it had been decided to try and keep it a secret from her father. They weren't very sure they could manage this, John being rather observant, but they thought it was worth a try.

'Do you think we dare count on good weather?' said her mother, glancing out of the conservatory windows. For the first time today there was a hint of autumn in the air, with wisps of mist in the valleys and an orangey tinge to the bracken.

'I don't think we can count on it,' said Rachel cautiously. The weather had improved since those two weeks of torrential rain, but the heat of the early summer was well and truly a thing of the past. 'I think we need to work out how many people we can cope with if we open up the conservatory through to the kitchen here. The sitting room is still a disaster area until the new carpets arrive.'

'Yes, I think we'll definitely leave the sitting room out of the equation. It's a lovely little room for the family, but even at the best of times you couldn't say it was spacious.'

'Your idea to add the conservatory was great,' said Rachel. 'It's made such a difference to the house. Now, how many people were you thinking of inviting?'

They spent the next half hour happily listing friends both local and from farther afield. Maggie was keen to invite her husband's brothers. His elder brother and his wife lived near Coventry and Rachel thought there was a good chance they would come, but she doubted very much if his rather wild younger brother would make it from France. Eventually they decided on a list of forty invitees, of whom less than thirty were realistically likely to attend.

'That's plenty,' said Rachel. 'Catering for that many will be a lot of work. I wonder if we should get in someone from outside.'

'No, said her mother with unexpected firmness. I'm not nearly as fragile as you think, Rachel. I've been enjoying getting back into cooking now you are taking on more of the outside work. I can prepare things over the next couple of weeks and freeze them. There'll be plenty.'

'If you're sure . . . '

'I'm sure. Now, as time is rather short I think we should phone people rather than send out invitations. I'll do family and we can maybe split the neighbours between us. I thought, for example, you could do the younger people, such as Philip Milligan.'

She left a pause and Rachel sighed. She really didn't know what had happened with Philip, why he had disappeared from their lives. She was concentrating on helping her parents making a go of the kennels. She didn't want to think about this annoying man, but if she mentioned that to her mother she would only worry.

'Yes, I'll phone him,' she said as brightly as she was able. 'Why don't you do a list of who you want me to contact and I'll make a start this afternoon when Dad is at the bowling.'

'That's a good idea,' said her mother. 'I'm so glad your father is well enough to get back to his bowls, he does enjoy it. You know, that ankle is almost as good as new. The hospital did an excellent job.'

'Let's hope they can do as good a one for you. When are you due back at the out-patients to have your medication reviewed?'

'Next week. But don't you worry about me, Rachel. You worry far too much about your parents. We're fine, and we're enjoying having you here, but you've got to think about getting on with your own life.'

Rachel was surprised. Her mother must be feeling a lot better if she was reverting to the bossy ways Rachel remembered from her teenage years. Maybe that's where Rachel got it from?

'My life's great,' she said, giving her mother a hug. 'Now I'm going to take Jim the Great Dane for a walk, and after lunch I'll start phoning.'

Most of the phone calls went very well. Rachel knew her parents' acquaintances from visits home over recent years, and was enjoying learning more about them now she had settled here for good. She chatted happily with all and sundry, confirming that the worst of the flood damage was now dealt with, that her father really didn't look sixty did he, and how pleasant it would be if they had a nice dry autumn. She left Philip Milligan until last. She really wasn't sure what to say to him.

'Milligan here,' he said on answering. His tones were clipped and reminded Rachel of how he had first appeared, remote and abrupt.

'Oh, Philip. It's Rachel.' She felt suddenly breathless.

'Ah. Rachel. How are you?'

'Fine. Keeping busy, you know. How are you? And Amelia?'

'We're both fine. We've been meaning to call in and see you, but, ah, never seemed quite the right time.'

'Amelia's still with you, is she?' asked Rachel, wondering exactly what he meant by those words.

'Goes back this week, as it happens.'

'Wish her all the best from me,' said Rachel. She would have liked to invite them round for a 'goodbye' tea, but was unsure how that would be received. 'I'm phoning up on my parents' behalf, actually. My father turns sixty in a couple of weeks' time and we're arranging a party for him. They wondered if you might be able to come?'

She told him the date and time, pleased with herself for issuing the invitation in her parents' name rather than her own.

'That's very kind of them,' said Philip in a cool voice that made her immediately fear the worst. 'I'm not sure I'll be back from down south. After I've dropped Amelia at her mother's I'm going on to London to see my agent. I've taken rather too long off this summer, time I was thinking about getting back to work.'

'The invitation's there if you're back in time,' said Rachel primly. 'I hope the trip goes well.'

She was left feeling empty after the phone call. It annoyed her. Why had Philip Milligan embarked on a friendship with her if he didn't mean to take it anywhere? And why on earth did she care? Definitely time to think about what she was going to do with her new life here, and what kind of dog she really wanted.

* * *

Anthony looked around Rupert Randall's workshop as though he were in

Aladdin's cave. This was his third visit, but he still hadn't taken it all in. Everything fascinated him, from the massive prints leaning against the back wall to the trays of tiny cutting knives. Even the smell, of glue and ink and he didn't know what else, was tantalising.

Rupert was bent over the work bench, engrossed in his cutting, and had merely grunted when Anthony appeared. Now he straightened to his not very considerable height.

'Good to see you. I've an order for twenty more of those Mountains at Dusk prints, I thought you could maybe run them off for me?'

Anthony nodded. So far he had only run off a print under Rupert's supervision. This was a step forward. And maybe, one day soon, he would be allowed to try some lino cuts of his own. He had been doodling with design ideas at the desk in his bedroom, but he hadn't shown those to anyone yet.

They worked in silence until Rupert decreed it was time for a coffee break.

They went over to the house for this, Rupert not willing to sully his workshop with kitchen paraphernalia.

'How's that nice young lady I met you with at the show?' he asked as they sat down at the tiny kitchen table.

'She's fine. She's off to college the day after tomorrow.' Anthony had been trying not to think about this.

'Art College?'

'No, she's doing Business Studies. She says it'll be interesting.'

'I could do with someone looking after the business side of things here for me,' said Rupert, rubbing his nose meditatively. 'My wife used to take care of that.'

'Your wife?' said Anthony. He hadn't thought of Rupert as the kind of person who married, had a family.

'Aye, Janie. She died two years ago. I still miss her.'

'I, er, sorry,' said Anthony.

The man shot him a brief smile from his dark little eyes. 'The house wasn't always such a mess, you know. I manage as well as I can, but there never seems to be time for everything. Especially not things like accounts and tax returns.'

Anthony shuddered at the thought of them. 'My sister seems to like doing things like that,' he said, still amazed that this could be true. 'She's taken over the accounts side of my parents' business. They're relieved and she says it suits her, putting figures neatly into columns. I supposes it is the kind of thing that would suit her. She does like everything to be organised.'

'If she's looking for a few hours work, tell her to pop round and see me,' said Rupert. 'It'd only be a couple of hours here and there but it would be a great help.'

'I'll mention it to her. I don't really know what she wants to do with herself. She's actually a teacher but I don't know if she's going to look for a job here. She used to live in Liverpool.'

'Aye, could tell none of you were local. She's a nice lass, your sister, I'm sure she'll find her feet all right.'

Anthony sighed, in no doubt that this was true. But when would he find his own feet? He was enjoying spending time with Rupert, loving it actually, but it wasn't going to lead anywhere, was it?

He left Rupert's at five and went home quickly to shower and change. Gemma had stopped working at the Boroughbie Arms the previous weekend and he had hardly seen her since. Tonight, to his secret surprise, she had agreed to go out to the movies with him, as a farewell. He was both looking forward to and dreading it.

He borrowed his mother's car and picked her up at the end of the farm track. As usual, he wasn't allowed to go up to the house.

'Let's not go to the movie,' said Gemma as the neared the town. 'Can we go somewhere to talk, instead?'

Anthony was delighted. He'd far rather spend time somewhere he could see her than in the dark of the movie house.

He took her to a little bar-café that had some tables in the garden. Gemma wasn't yet eighteen and he suddenly felt protective, not keen to take her into a rowdy bar. He was relieved when she asked for a fruit juice. He chose a shandy for himself, as he was driving.

'This is a nice place,' said Gemma, looking around the small but sunny garden. 'I've never been before.'

Anthony wasn't surprised. Her father wasn't the sort who would take her out or encourage her to go with friends.

'So how does it feel, just about to venture out in to the big wide world?' he asked encouragingly. For all her suggestion they go somewhere to talk, she was now very quiet.

'I'm worried about Dad,' she said, turning the glass round and round in her hands. 'He's really miserable about me going. He doesn't say much, but I know he's dreading it.'

Anthony didn't want her to go away either but now he felt immensely irritated with this man.

'It's your life, you've got to live it. He can't keep you at home for ever.'

'I know. And I've told him that I'll come home as many weekends as I can, and every holiday. And once I graduate I can come back home to live, like your sister, Rachel, has done.'

Anthony was sure Rachel had come home to suit herself rather than her parents, but he didn't say so. He wondered where he would be in four years time, if and when Gemma returned.

'Surely he wants you to get good qualifications,' he said rallyingly. 'You said he was pleased with your exam results.'

'But he's going to be so lonely when I'm away. And I help a bit round the farm, he's going to miss that too.'

'He'll just have to get someone in to do it,' said Anthony. It seemed quite obvious to him.

'Yes, that's what I thought.' Gemma hesitated, glancing at him from beneath lowered lashes. 'The thing is, I was wondering. I know you've got a part-time job at the hotel, and you're helping Rupert Randall out a bit, but I wondered if you'd like another part-time job — a bit closer to home.'

Anthony looked at her aghast. She couldn't be suggesting what he thought she was suggesting. 'I hardly know your father. And you have to admit it, he doesn't like me.'

'That's because he doesn't know you, like you said. This is a way for him to get to know you.' Gemma's tone was triumphant now. 'Everyone you've worked for is really pleased with you.'

'Once Mrs Mackenzie got over her shock at me arguing with her customers.'

'And once Dad gets to know you I'm sure he'll like you. And I'd worry less about him, if I knew you were round there once or twice a week.'

Anthony was flabbergasted. He wanted to do something to please Gemma, but he really couldn't see this working out.

'And what does your father think?' he

asked cautiously. It would be much easier if Gemma's father put an end to the idea, then he wouldn't be the one turning her down.

'I haven't mentioned it to him yet. I thought I should speak to you first.'

'But I don't know anything about farming, I'm not sure I'd be any use.' Anthony was prevaricating now.

'You're good with animals, at least you are with the dogs. And you're strong. And quite sensible.' She grinned at him as she said that which made his heart do a little flip. 'More sensible than you used to be. You'd just need to do whatever he told you. You can drive a car so you'd manage the tractor no problem.'

'You drive the tractor?' said Anthony, impressed.

'Yes, I told you, I have to help where I can. When Mum was alive we had a bigger place and they both farmed it together . . . Dad hasn't always been so solitary, you know.'

They sat in silence for a moment.

Gemma sipped her drink, her expression sad now because she had mentioned her mother.

'What happened to your mother?' asked Anthony tentatively. No-one seemed to know and Gemma never spoke about it.

'She died of septicaemia.'

'Of . . . ?' Anthony wracked his brains to recall what this was. 'Like an infection?'

'Yes. A bad one. Blood poisoning, Dad calls it.'

'How did she get that?'

Gemma lowered her head so that the long hair fell across her face. 'It was a dog bite. Stupid, isn't it?' She was trying to keep her tone light but she didn't look up. 'There were some stray dogs near where we used to live. They hung around the farm sometimes. I thought they were sweet and I tried to stroke one but . . . well, it went for me and cornered me in the yard. Mum came out to see what the noise was. When she tried to help me it went for her.' Anthony was sure she was close to tears.

'You don't need to tell me if you don't want.'

She continued as though he hadn't spoken. 'She wasn't really that badly bitten, either. The dogs ran off and she got us both into the kitchen and cleaned up our wounds. Little scratches, she called them, said she'd had far worse before. She wouldn't go and see a doctor, even when her hand started swelling up. Eventually she was getting these awful fevers and Dad took her to hospital, but it was too late. They gave her all sorts of antibiotics and I don't know what but she died anyway. Stupid, isn't it? From a little dog bite.'

'So that's why your father doesn't like dogs,' said Anthony. For the first time the fury on the man's face whenever he met him whilst walking the kennel occupants made sense.

'It wasn't the dog's fault, it was my fault. But Dad won't see that.'

'It wasn't anyone's fault,' said Anthony.

'Sounds like it was just incredibly bad luck. And if your mum hadn't been so tough and not gone to the doctor . . . '

'That was just the way she was. She was brilliant, very brave.' Gemma gave him a watery smile and delved in her bag for a tissue. 'So you can understand why Dad is so protective of me.'

Anthony nodded. He could certainly understand that. The whole bizarre series of events would have made her father very wary indeed.

'But I think that's all the more reason why he wouldn't want me around,' he said. He wasn't trying to get out of it now, just being honest. 'No wonder he hates anything to do with kennels. And seeing me would just remind him of it.'

'Don't you see? I've been thinking about it. The best thing for him to do is face up to the fact that his hatred of dogs is absurd. If he can realise that, then maybe he can get back to living some kind of normal life.'

'And then you could too,' said Anthony.

'I'm not thinking about me.'

'I know you're not, but it's true.'

'So will you help?' She nudged his hand where it lay on the table and he immediately took the opportunity to hold on to hers.

'I don't really see how . . . '

'I've got this brilliant idea. He's been invited to your father's sixtieth birthday party. Your mum's been very good at inviting him to things although he never goes. Of course, he doesn't want to go to this either, but if I say I'll come home from uni for the weekends, specially, I think I might be able to persuade him. Then I'll be able to introduce him to you, properly, and he'll see what a brilliant place your kennels are and . . . Well, we can take it from there.'

'It's an idea,' said Anthony doubtfully. And as he didn't have anything better to suggest, they agreed on this as their plan.

Philip Confides In Alison

Philip was on his way to his sister's. It was ten weeks since he had made that last trip down here and so much had happened in the meantime he didn't feel like the same person. For a start, he was looking forward to seeing Alison and telling her all that he and Amelia had been doing. And then he also wanted to ask her advice.

He had thought there was no one he could talk to about his confused feelings for Rachel Collington, and then he realised there was Alison.

They had been getting on so much better during the frequent phone conversations, he felt he really knew his sister for the first time. She no longer seemed an intrusive older sister, just someone who cared about him and who he cared about.

'Do you think Daddy will be home

too?' asked Amelia from the back seat, for at least the third time.

'No, I'm sure he won't. Remember that was one of the reasons your mum had to stay so long in Dubai, because she wasn't well enough to travel unaccompanied and your dad couldn't get any more time off to bring her home.'

'Oh, yes.'

'But it'll be great to see your mum, won't it? And I'm sure your dad will be home as soon as he can.' Philip couldn't understand how Colin could bear to be away from his daughter for such long periods of time. He was going to miss her terribly when he returned to Courockglen without her.

'I wish we could have brought Bill and Ben to meet Mum,' said Amelia, returning to another of her pet subjects.

'They might have been a bit too boisterous for your mum just now,' said Philip judiciously. 'All the more reason for you to persuade her to bring you to visit me soon. She can meet them then.'

'They would have liked to come with us,' said Amelia sadly.

It was true that Bill and Ben had jumped into the car with alacrity when they had seen the bags being loaded, but they had been equally happy to be dropped off at Collington Kennels. Philip hadn't timed the visit specifically to avoid seeing Rachel, but he had been relieved that he managed to do so.

'They don't like long car journeys,' was all he said. 'Now, why don't you use my mobile to phone your mum and tell her we'll be with her in about half-an-hour?'

Alison looked surprisingly well. Amelia flew out of the car and into her mother's arms which gave Philip a moment to take in his sister's appearance. She looked tanned and relaxed. She might even have put on a little weight, which wouldn't be a bad thing. Her hair and clothes were as neat as ever, but she wore less make up and her smile was brighter.

'You're looking great,' he said, giving

her an affectionate hug.

He carried their bags inside, Amelia chattering ten to the dozen. She had clearly enjoyed her time with her uncle, but she was just as clearly delighted to be home. She ran up to her room to check on her toys and Alison put on the kettle.

'Tea or coffee?' she said. 'Or something stronger?'

'A bit early in the day for that,' said Philip, amazed at this departure from the norm.

'What does it matter? We're celebrating. One of the neighbours popped in with a bottle of champagne, wasn't that good of her? I've been dying to have someone to share it with, let's open it.'

'Well, if you put it like that . . . ' said Philip. He had the feeling he was going to enjoy this visit. Alison was so grateful to him for looking after Amelia — as she should be — but it was more than that, she really seemed like a different person.

He opened the bottle and Alison

found lemonade for Amelia and they all said cheers to a happy and healthy future. A little later, when Amelia had settled in a corner surrounded by her dolls, Philip said softly to his sister, 'You were ill for quite a while, weren't you?'

Alison nodded slowly. 'Yes. For years. I hadn't realised, it came on so gradually, but I was getting weaker and weaker and moodier and moodier. Apparently a lot of that was hormones and now they've put it right I feel like a new woman.' She smiled, a clear and happy smile and he realised it was years since he had seen her smile like that. 'I must have been awful to be around. I'm so much happier now.'

'I'm so glad.'

'So am I. So is Colin. And we've taken a big decision.' She lowered her voice. 'I don't want to tell Melie until we know for sure it is going to work out, but Colin is hoping to give up his job in Dubai at the end of the year and come home. Any job he gets here won't pay so well, but we've decided it's more important for all the family to be together. Nice as it is out there, it's not where we want to bring Amelia up.'

'That's brilliant news,' said Philip. 'Amelia missed you, obviously, when she was with me. But she missed Colin too. She'll be so pleased.'

★　★　★

They spent a very pleasant evening preparing a light meal and chatting, catching up on so many things that Philip hadn't thought he was interested in but now found he was. Colin's life out in the Middle East, Alison's early memories of their parents that he hadn't shared, her certainty that they had been proud of the little success he had achieved before their deaths. He was amazed how much she knew about his career, how avidly she had followed it.

Alison took a long time over putting Amelia to bed. Philip wasn't surprised. The two had been everything to each other for a long time, and this separation hadn't been easy for either of them.

It warmed him to see how happy they were to be together again. He sat and sipped his coffee and mused over the intricacies of family relationships.

'I bet you'll be glad to get home and have a bit of peace,' said Alison when she came back down to join him. They were sitting in the living room. It was decorated, like the kitchen, in very pale tones, but someone had sent Alison flowers, and they made a happy splash of red against the creams and whites. Philip wished he had thought to send or bring flowers.

'It'll seem very quiet without Amelia,' he said. 'To be honest, I'm going to miss her, and the dogs certainly are.'

'It's clear she's going to miss them.'

'All the more reason to bring her up for a visit.'

'I'd like that. Maybe I'll get to meet this Rachel that Amelia has spoken so much about.'

'Ah. Yes.' Philip remembered he had wanted to discuss Rachel with his sister, but now the opportunity had presented itself he didn't know what to say. 'Her family own the boarding kennels where Bill and Ben were staying. Very nice family.'

'Is she pretty?' asked Alison, head on one side.

'Yes, she's pretty. But that's not the main thing you notice about her. She's so — bright and bubbly, so involved in life.'

'And you like that?'

Philip realised it must seem strange, that someone as reserved as he was should be drawn to such a girl. 'I like her. I think. But we're very different. I don't really understand her. She has this fierce loyalty to her parents and her brother. I don't know if she has room for anyone else in her life.'

'Then you'll have to find out,' said Alison lightly.

She rose to switch on some of the side lamps. The nights were starting to draw in. 'If you are interested enough to make the effort.'

Philip felt something shiver inside him. He was afraid. Afraid of what it might mean, if he put himself out to get closer to Rachel. What if she rejected him? He would be opening himself up to being hurt.

'She's probably not interested in me.'

'From the things Melie has said, it sounds like she might be. And you know, you're quite an attractive man, or so all my friends tell me. Why wouldn't she be interested?'

Philip smiled at the backhanded compliment. 'She doesn't seem to be interested in money or status or any of those things.'

'Good. So if she likes you it'll be for yourself. I think you should get back up there and find out.'

'Maybe I will,' said Philip. He was pleased to have the encouragement, but still unwilling to commit himself. 'But first I have to go down to London to see my agent. I'll need to leave first thing in the morning if I'm not going to be late so I think I'll head off to bed now.'

'Good idea,' said Alison with a delicate yawn. She didn't try to push him further about Rachel. Amazingly, she seemed to trust him to make the right decision for himself.

* * *

John Collington came through to the kitchen after taking a phone call in the little room they called the office. He sat down heavily at the table.

'That's another cancellation. Acquaintances of Pixie's owners, from what I can gather. Said they'd heard the kennels weren't back up to full strength after the recent floods and they didn't want to inconvenience us by bringing their two dogs here.'

'Didn't you tell them everything is perfectly all right?' demanded Rachel indignantly.

'Of course. But they didn't want to

hear that. If people want to cancel, we can't stop them, can we?'

'That means we're only half full for the next fortnight,' said his wife sadly. 'We haven't been this quiet over a summer and autumn since the first year we opened.'

When her father went back outside after his tea break Rachel followed him. It broke her heart to see him so depressed by this news. Things had been going relatively well. The slight flood-damage to the kennels had long since been sorted and he had been enjoying himself enlarging the runs and tidying the garden, saying when they weren't so busy was the ideal time to do this. Now this one cancellation seemed to have taken the wind right out of his sails.

'It's such a shame, I can't understand it,' she said, leaning against the wall. Her father began to dig lethargically.

'These things happen. Perhaps we were in the wrong and should have explained more about what had happened to Pixie's owners.'

'If you remember, you were going to, but they were in a great hurry when they picked her up and there wasn't the chance.' Rachel frowned. 'I'm going to find out what is going on here. Who is starting this whispering campaign about the kennels? I'm convinced it hasn't just happened by accident.'

Her father didn't seem interested. 'We should have made more effort to speak to all the dog owners. Still, it's a lesson for the future. If we are to have a future here. I'm starting to think maybe now would be a good time to sell up and retire properly.'

'Dad! You can't do that.'

'This business was supposed to be something we were doing for fun. Now, with your mother's health not so good, and all the other little problems, maybe we have to be realistic. We always planned to move into a smaller house in Boroughbie at some stage. Maybe that time has come a little sooner than we expected.'

Rachel was horrified. 'But you love it

here! And think of all the people who rely on you to look after their dogs. For all your problems, you've built up quite a regular clientele. And Mum likes the space and quiet.'

'But she'd also like to be in walking distance of the shops. She's finding it more and more difficult to drive and it would be nice for her not to have to rely on me. Or you.'

'I don't mind. I love being here.'

'You've been a great help, Rachel, but this was our plan, not yours. You need to think what you want to do with your life for yourself.' He left the trowel standing in the damp soil and turned to look directly at her for the first time. He smiled sadly, the laughter lines no longer seeming a sign of cheer. 'It's not only Anthony who doesn't seem to know what to do with his life.'

'But . . . ' said Rachel. She couldn't understand how this conversation had turned round and now seemed to be about her. 'I'm loving being here.'

'And as I said, we love having you.

But this could only ever be a temporary arrangement. Your mother and I enjoy having both our children at home just now, but we've always known that you'll grow up and move on to live your own lives one day. We're quite happy with that. We've got each other.'

Rachel met his eyes and felt guilty. She had thought she was the one being helpful here, doing the right thing, which just happened to suit what she wanted to do. Now she wondered for the first time if her parents resented her coming home. She felt her heart sink and a great hollow feeling envelope her.

'I'm in the way, aren't I?'

'No, my dear, you will never be in the way. We love having you here. But in the long run we want to see you settled doing something you want to do, not helping us do something we want to do.'

There was a familiar ring to these words. Rachel seemed to remember saying something very similar to Anthony. Why had she not realised that they applied to her, too?

'I never took a gap year,' she said at last. 'Surely I'm allowed to have one year out, to see how it feels?'

'Rachel, you're allowed to have as long an 'out' as you want. You work too hard, taking a proper break would do you good. But in the long run, only you can know what it really is you want to do with your life.'

When Rachel left her father she took two of the dogs and headed up into the hills. Her feelings were too confused to return to the house and her mother. This was the most serious conversation she could remember ever having with her father. She was shaken, not just by what he had said, but that he had made the effort to say it. He seemed to think she needed advice, just as much as she thought everyone else did.

The higher she climbed through the crisp autumn grass the clearer one thing became. Before she could think about her future, she needed to find out what was causing her parents' problems. It was the sight of the new earth works that made her decide this. She examined them closely, keeping the dogs firmly on their leads but nevertheless expecting farmer Freddy Smith to appear over the brow of a hill, shouting at her.

The digger had disappeared but from what she could see new trenches had been dug to drain water from the upper slopes. And they all drained into the Inshie Burn. Strange how that coincided with the first time the burn had flooded. She thought it was about time she tackled Freddy Smith on this issue, and maybe one or two others as well.

Once she had done that, maybe it would be time to move on.

* * *

Philip returned from London filled with a new sense of purpose. Not only had his agent been very positive about the first draft of his book, but there was a good chance the television series would be commissioned for another season.

He thought one further run would be about the right time to draw it to a conclusion.

As he drove the winding stretch of road towards Collington Kennels his spirits rose. He couldn't be sure, of course, that Rachel would be there, but just the possibility of seeing her made his heart race a little faster. He was still afraid of what might happen if he opened himself up to this beautiful girl, but he was determined now to take the risk.

It was Maggie Collington who opened the door to him. She shook his hand warmly. 'Lovely to see you again. You will stay and have a cup of tea, won't you? I've just baked a Victoria sponge, it would be a shame not to cut in to it while it's fresh. I'll let John know you're here and he can bring Bill and Ben down. They've been very good, such happy dogs . . . '

Philip allowed himself to be ushered in to the kitchen and let the chatter wash over him. He was happy the dogs were in good health, not that he had expected anything different. He knew the Collingtons well enough by now to realise that whatever rumours were going around about the kennels were pure fabrication. What he really wanted to know was the whereabouts of Rachel. He was sure if he waited long enough he would find out and sure enough Maggie soon moved on to this subject.

'Rachel will be so sorry she missed you. She's gone to Edinburgh for the day. She and an old school friend have been trying to arrange to meet up for a while and eventually they managed it. I'm so pleased for her, she deserves a day out. Edinburgh is a lovely city, isn't it? Do you know it well yourself?'

Philip hid his disappointment and managed to engage in a discussion of the attractions of Edinburgh. He liked Maggie Collington, but was more at ease with her husband. Once John joined them the conversation turned immediately to more interesting things, such as the plans to re-enact a medieval battle in the grounds of a local tower house. Philip had realised that if he was to live in this area there was no way out of being involved in such local events, and he had found himself on the organising committee.

'So good of you to give up your time,' said John Collington.

'I'm enjoying it,' said Philip, which, to his surprise, was true. 'I've never been involved with re-enactments before and the house in question has a really interesting history of its own. In fact, please don't mention it to anyone, but we're hoping to feature it in my new series, all being well.'

Yes, it was pleasant to sit and chat with the Collingtons. It was silly of him to have avoided them for the last few weeks.

Maggie walked with him to the door. Her movements seemed rather stiff, but she was as cheerful as ever.

'I'm so glad you're back before the weekend,' she said in a lowered voice.

'You haven't forgotten it's the party for John's sixtieth? I know Rachel said you might not be able to come if you were away, but now you're home we'd love to see you.'

Philip smiled and nodded his acceptance. Here was a definite date for seeing Rachel again.

A Nasty Confrontation

The morning of John's party dawned bright and clear. It wasn't his actual birthday until the Sunday, but it had been decided to have the party on the Saturday. Maggie went over all the arrangements in her head as she waited for John to bring up her morning cup of tea. He had got into this habit when she hadn't been well and it was a rather nice routine.

The few minutes solitude gave her a chance to check off everything in her mind. The food had been prepared gradually over the weeks and was now defrosting on the pantry shelves. Rachel had arranged the hire of glasses and plates. Anthony would go with her to collect drinks that morning. Balloons would be put up at the last minute, if they could manage to get John out of the way as planned.

If the weather stayed like this, it was going to be fantastic.

John brought up tea on a tray. She was pleased to see he had brought a cup for himself, which meant he wasn't going straight out to work.

'Lovely morning,' he said, nodding at the high white clouds in the sky.

'I do hope it stays like this,' said Maggie and then, when he gave her a puzzled look, wished she hadn't.

He sat down on the edge of the bed. 'Maggie, my dear, do you mind if I ask you something?'

'No,' said Maggie. He suspected something, she was sure of it.

'Are you going to tell me what's going on?'

'Goodness, whatever do you mean?'

'Now, Mags, you know you were never very good at keeping a secret. And there has been just a little too much whispering and knowing looks between you and the children.'

Maggie was sure her face must have fallen. 'I don't know what you're talking about,' she said, but she knew she would never carry it off now.

He patted her hand, smiling across at her affectionately. 'The final clue was the amount of food I've just spotted in the pantry. Enough to feed the five thousand, I would have said.'

'You weren't supposed to look in the pantry!' Maggie protested. 'You never go in there.'

'I wanted to bring you some biscuits up, as a Saturday treat,' he said, indicating the plate on the tray. 'And I've had my suspicions for a while. It's a party for my sixtieth, isn't it?'

Maggie sighed. She had been enjoying the excitement of these secret preparations. 'Yes. It was Anthony's idea, actually. You don't mind, do you? We wanted to make it a special time for you.'

'Of course I don't mind! I'm delighted. No need to tell the children I know, but if you just explain the arrangements to me I'll make sure all the chores are done in time. Then I can get out of your way at the appropriate moment.'

'Yes, that might make things easier,' said Maggie, cheering up again.

★   ★   ★

Anthony waited impatiently for Gemma and her father to arrive. He hadn't seen her since she went away a fortnight ago. She had texted him to say her father had agreed to come to the party, all being well, but when he questioned his mother she said there had been no acceptance of the invitation, so he was left on tenterhooks.

The day had started dry but windy and Rachel and their mother were fussing over the best way to pin down tablecloths and the dangers of using plastic cups in this weather. He really didn't see that any of these things were important. His dad had been persuaded surprisingly easily to go and collect the Saturday papers and do one or two other errands. The decorations were up and the first visitors had begun to appear.

But where was Gemma?

She still hadn't arrived when the word came that his father's car was approaching. The visitors were crowded into the conservatory, although how his father wasn't going to suspect something with the number of vehicles out the front he didn't know. Still, he went along with it, holding the doors closed until Rachel gave the signal and then throwing them open to a great bang of party poppers, clapping and laughing.

His father looked momentarily nonplussed, his cheerful face suffused with colour as he saw all the people.

'Happy birthday, John!' shouted someone from the back.

'Happy sixtieth!' shouted someone else.

'I bet you didn't expect to see us here,' said his father's sister-in-law, coming forward to hug him.

His father shook his head, slowly, and met his brother's eyes when he said,

'No, I really didn't. Some of you have travelled miles. I'm quite overcome.'

His wife hustled him forward as he seemed, for once, to have forgotten his easy social skills. 'Here, Rachel has a glass for you, and then you can come and say hello to everyone.'

The party began in earnest then, with only the one or two late arrivals drifting in. Anthony thought he was going to get a crick in his neck, he swung round so often to see who was coming through the door. And then, suddenly, Gemma and her father were there. Maggie spotted them and immediately made to draw them forward, apparently delighted to see them.

She wasn't the only one. Anthony was at Gemma's side in an instant. 'I'll get drinks,' he said. 'What would you like?'

It was only when Anthony returned with the drinks and had the chance to look more closely at Gemma that he realised all was not well. He found it hard to judge Freddy Smith's expression, as he was always so grim, but

Gemma looked ready to cry.

This wasn't right. Anthony said bracingly, 'How are you getting on at university? Fresher's Week go OK?' He thought it best that her father didn't know they'd been exchanging text messages.

'Yes, thank you. It was good.'

'Too much drinking and making fools of themselves,' said her father sourly, frowning at his daughter. 'I hope you didn't have any part in that.'

'No, Dad. I said, it was just the fun things.'

'Hmm.' Her father looked around at the groups of happy, chattering people. His expression made it all too clear that he didn't approve of such frivolity.

Anthony wondered how on earth Gemma had persuaded her father to come here, and how long they were likely to stay. Not very long, from the way the man was already looking at his watch.

'I'm worried about that new bull. I really need to get back.'

'Dad, you said you'd stay for a bit.' Gemma bit her lip.

Anthony flashed her a smile, to show he was on her side, and it seemed to cheer her a little. She smiled briefly back and then took a deep breath and touched her father on the arm.

'Dad, I've been thinking.'

'Hmm?'

'You know how busy you are around the farm, now I'm not home to help.'

'I don't begrudge you going. I'm not one to make my children stay home and run their business for them.'

'No, I know that, Dad. But I was thinking, it would be useful for you to have a hand every now and then, wouldn't it? And Anthony here is living nearby and I wondered if he might be willing to help out . . . ?'

Freddy looked at Anthony as though he had never seen him before, and would rather it had stayed that way. 'Aren't you going to college, boy?'

'No, I, er, decided not to.'

'Why? I can't see there's anything to

keep you here.' The way Freddy looked around his parents pretty, tidy home made Anthony seethe. This was a great place!

Gemma spoke quickly before he could say something out of turn. 'Anthony is working with a local artist. Rupert Randall. He's quite well known and he's taken on Anthony as a kind of apprentice.'

Anthony felt this was stretching the truth a little, but was flattered all the same.

'You don't look the arty type,' said Freddy, looking him up and down.

'How would you feel about doing a bit of work for my dad?' Gemma asked Anthony, as though they hadn't discussed this before. 'It would be a real help to us.'

'I'm managing fine,' said her father abruptly.

'I wouldn't mind,' said Anthony. He thought he would mind, a lot. But if Gemma wanted him to give it a try he would.

'Anthony's very good with animals,' said Gemma encouragingly. 'He does a lot with the dogs here, as you can imagine.'

'Ah, dogs.' Her father's expression turned from annoyance to anger in a second. 'Yes, your family are all very good with dogs, aren't they? Can't keep them under control, can't keep their owners happy. That's what I hear. Don't know why you bother anyway. Nasty, useless beasts, so they are.'

* * *

Rachel had been eyeing Freddy Smith from a distance. She didn't want to cause a scene at her father's party, but it did seem like a good opportunity to have a word with him, when he couldn't actually refuse to speak to her. Gemma and Anthony seemed to be trying to engage him in conversation themselves, but whatever it was they were discussing didn't seem to be finding favour with the man.

She had been avoiding Philip Milligan by the simple expedient of moving to the farther side of the pantry from wherever he happened to be. Now she spotted him heading towards her and decided to join Freddy's little group. She was just in time to hear him spitting out something about dogs.

His tone was furious and he glared at the line of kennels with such venom that Rachel almost quailed.

Then she realised this was just the opportunity she was waiting for.

'Is that our kennels you're discussing?' she asked pleasantly.

All three of the little group jumped at the sound of her voice, so engrossed were they in their own discussion.

Anthony gave her a meaningful look she couldn't interpret. 'We're fine, just having a little chat.'

Freddy Smith turned to Rachel. 'I was just saying I don't know why you bother with a business like this. What good does it do anyone? It's not like you're producing anything, are you?'

'My parents provide a very valuable service to dog owners,' replied Rachel.

'Providing a luxury for a luxury. What do these people want dogs for? It's not as if they're working animals. At least there is a reason for a good sheepdog . . . '

'Not that we've even got a sheepdog,' said Gemma, interrupting before he could get into full flow. 'I would have quite liked one, but . . . '

Anthony nodded to her, as though he understood what she was saying. None of it made any sense to Rachel.

'Mr Smith,' she said, waiting for the man to meet her eyes. 'Can I ask you something?'

'Ask? Ask? Ask away for all I care.' All the same, the man seemed uncomfortable now, aware they were attracting attention.

'I want to know whether you might have done anything that might have, ah, been detrimental to the kennels? You know, caused us one or two problems?' Rachel was playing this by ear.

'I don't know what you're talking about.'

She said carefully, 'The drainage work you've been doing, for a start. That directed an awful lot more water than usual into the Inshie Burn and you must have realised that it would all come down this way.'

'The Inshie Burn? Are you saying I caused that flood? If I had so much control over the weather, believe me, I'd be delighted. But I can't control a freak of nature. Anyone would know that.'

'And that's not the only thing,' continued Rachel, determined now to see this through. 'What about the surprise visit from the animal welfare people? Someone must have put them on to that.'

'I know when I see an animal not being looked after properly. All that barking, stands to reason there were problems here.'

Rachel stared at him. 'So it was you!'

'Only doing my duty,' he hissed back, ignoring the gasp from his daughter. 'If everything was being run properly here you would have had nothing to worry about.'

'We did have nothing to worry about. The inspectors were perfectly happy! But it really upset my parents.'

'They should have thought about that,' said the man grimly. 'Running the kennels is one thing, but taking in strays is bound to start people talking.'

Rachel shook her head, amazed at what she was hearing. 'So all the bad publicity we've been getting, all the rumours, they didn't just happen, did they? It was you!'

Rachel could see Philip Milligan approaching from one side and her father from the other but she couldn't stop now. 'What have you got to say about that, Mr Smith?'

Freddy caught sight of the tall, dark figure of Philip and his eyes narrowed. 'It wasn't me that told the world about your kennels being flooded out, scaring the daylights out of your soft dog owners. It was your friend here. He's the one who has been spreading rumours, if that's what you want to call them.'

Anthony, Gemma and Rachel all swung round to Philip. Rachel expected an instant denial but instead Philip hesitated. He was definitely looking uncomfortable. 'Yes, well, it wasn't quite like that.'

'You caused us all those problems with Pixie's owners?' Rachel couldn't believe it.

'So you see, I'm not the only one who has problems with this so-called business of yours,' said Freddy. He seemed relieved now he wasn't the one under the spotlight of Rachel's attention. 'Don't you try to blame it all on me.'

Whatever Rachel had expected from the celebration to mark her father's sixtieth, it wasn't this. She was stunned. Freddy Smith was clearly in some way connected with the kennels difficulties, he hadn't denied that. But to think it was Philip who had caused the latest blow that had hit her father so cruelly. She couldn't believe it. She had thought he was their friend, she really had.

'I can explain,' said Philip, still looking horrified.

'I need to go,' said Rachel. 'Food . . . Mum needs help . . . Please excuse me.' She ducked back into the house before anyone could stop her.

Freddy Was Very Brave

Philip couldn't believe he was making such a mess of things. He had returned from London with high hopes for the future. Suddenly it all seemed to have evaporated. Rachel wasn't speaking to him. Her parents, although polite as ever, were clearly hurt. And despite the fact he had been looking forward to having the house to himself again it felt lonely, no longer like home.

He took Bill and Ben for a walk through the early morning mist to try and clear his head. It was beautiful, with the leaves of the trees turning from rich greens to golden yellows and fiery reds, but his heart wasn't able to appreciate it.

He couldn't focus on anything except the feeling that everything was going wrong. And the more he thought about it, the more all his — and the

Collingtons' — difficulties seemed to involve Freddy Smith. There was only one thing for it, to beard the man himself and sort it out.

He was going to take Bill and Ben with him, but remembered at the last minute the farmer's strange dislike of dogs. He hugged them and apologised for leaving them behind and set off alone.

★   ★   ★

Inshie Heights Farm was set higher on the hillside than the Collingtons' cottage which was hidden from it by a line of trees. It was a medium-sized building, tidily maintained but without a homely touch. Philip wasn't sure what was lacking, but something was.

Philip parked his four-by-four at the front of the house and rang the bell. There was no response. He went around to the kitchen door and knocked. Still no response. Then he paused and listened to what might have been the sound of a quad bike. Yes, and it was becoming louder. Freddy must have been out in the fields but with a bit of luck he was on his way back. Philip strode to the foot of the track and waited.

Freddy would have been able to see him for a while as he descended the rough road, but he made no gesture of greeting. When he reached him he paused the vehicle but didn't turn off the engine. 'Aye? What can I do for you?'

'I wondered if we could have a chat?'

The farmer narrowed his eyes, displeased. Philip waited. He could be patient.

'I don't know that I've anything to say to you. Unless it's about the car accident. Did they ever find the blighter that bashed you?'

Philip had forgotten all about that. He had other things on his mind. He said reluctantly, 'It's not about that, although I should have thanked you for your help. And yes, they did find the other vehicle. The police had a word with the man and he decided to come clean, so I can claim off his insurance and not my own. A very good outcome.'

'That's the way it should be,' said Freddy, mellowing slightly. He nodded. 'Come on down, if you want to talk.' He pressed the accelerator and swung the quad bike away, not waiting for an answer.

Philip followed him more slowly, wondering now what exactly it was he wanted to say.

Freddy didn't take him into the house. He stowed the quad in a lean-to shed and then leant on the wall beside it.

'You must be missing your daughter, she's away at university now, isn't she?' Philip said, trying to break the ice.

'I manage fine. Nice to have a bit of peace, no more of this running backwards and forwards into town.'

'Yes, peace can be good,' said Philip encouragingly. 'That's why I moved to this part of the country myself. Lovely quiet corner, almost unknown compared to the Highlands.' Freddy had begun to move off now, closing one of the doors to a barn, checking on the contents of another. Philip followed him.

'Whether it's quiet or not depends on your neighbours, doesn't it?' said Freddy eventually.

This was just the opening Philip was hoping for. 'I would have said you're very lucky with your neighbours. A very nice family, the Collingtons.'

'I've nothing against the family,' said Freddy grudgingly. 'But that damn silly business they're running there is the problem. It's an eyesore, not to mention the noise.'

Philip remembered listening as he waited for Freddy to appear. He hadn't heard a single bark. 'I'd say an eyesore is the last thing it is,' he said mildly. 'I think the whole set up is very attractive. I really don't know what you've got against them.'

Freddy glared now, his dark face

taking on an even grimmer light. 'I came here to get away from things, didn't I? Came to make a new start for Gemma and me. The last thing I needed was something like that on my doorstep, reminding me.'

'Reminding you?' Philip was puzzled.

'Everyone thinks those Collingtons are so wonderful, taking in rescue dogs, joining every committee in town. I can see you're taken with them too, aren't you? Especially that pretty young woman. You'd better watch out for her, always meddling where she's not wanted.'

'Rachel doesn't meddle,' said Philip, wondering if that was quite true. Freddy had moved off again, towards the slurry pit this time, and he hurried after him. 'Look, I'm sorry you don't really like them as neighbours. But surely that's no reason to cause them difficulties? They're just trying to make a living like anyone else. And Maggie Collington hasn't been well. It's a shame if she has to worry.'

'Nobody worries about me, do they?' said Freddy, raising his voice now. He straightened a rusty sign that said *Danger* with an abrupt gesture. 'The Collingtons have got each other. Nobody cares that I lost my wife, for no reason, no reason at all.'

'I'm sorry . . . ' said Philip, stunned by this turn in the conversation.

'Everyone's sorry, they all say they're sorry, but that doesn't help, does it? I just don't want to be reminded, don't you understand? I can't bear to be reminded!' Freddy took hold of Philip's arm, shaking him quite violently as though this would make him understand.

Philip took a step back and suddenly found the ground beneath his feet giving way. They were on the very edge of the slurry pit, and Philip had his eyes on the other man, not on where he was standing.

He could feel himself slipping and then he was falling down, down, towards the dark liquid and that awful stench.

Rachel had gone to the Dog Rescue Centre near Dumfries with a box of food from her mother. Clients quite often brought their dogs' own food to the kennels and just as often declined to take any surplus away. The Collingtons passed this on to the Rescue Centre, along with, Rachel suspected, quite a bit they had paid for themselves.

Rachel always enjoyed a visit to the Centre, situated as it was on the slopes above the Solway Firth. The views were spectacular but most of all she loved the people who ran the place and the wonderful spirit that kept them going with very little funding and far too many unwanted dogs. How could there be such a thing as an unwanted dog? The very thought was appalling.

She had a cup of tea with Faye and agreed to ask her mum to bake some cakes for the upcoming Bring and Buy sale.

'We really need some more income,'

said the older woman with a sigh. 'Not that I ever know quite how much money we have coming in and going out. I wish I was better with the book-keeping.'

'Maybe I can help,' said Rachel. The centre was too far from the Kennels for her to do much practical work for them, but this was something she could do in her own time. 'Strange as it seems, I quite enjoy tidying up people's accounts. I'm doing Mum and Dad's, and I've just agreed to have a look at the books of an artist who lives in Boroughbie, Rupert Randall. Why don't I see if I can do something with yours, too?'

'That would be wonderful. But we couldn't pay you . . . '

'I wouldn't expect you to. It'll be my contribution to the Centre. And to tell you the truth, it's something I enjoy. It's amazing how satisfying it is to put everything neatly in the right column.'

Faye looked at her as if she was mad. Maybe she was. But it was true, Rachel really did enjoy this sort of work. She liked things to be tidy, organised. It was a shame her life couldn't be so easily sorted out.

Before she left, Faye invited her to walk around the kennels to see what dogs they had in.

'I'm in a bit of a hurry . . . ' began Rachel. That wasn't her real reason. Her real reason was that it broke her heart to see all the various waifs and strays, some desperate for affection, others cowering at the back of their cages.

'Come on, we've got a couple of new darlings in you won't have seen before.' Faye was good at not taking no for an answer. 'We've yet another Staffie, see, in the first kennel there? but I think we've got a home for him. But this one is a very sad case. This is Sally. She's a collie-cross. You're a sweetie, aren't you, darling?'

The dog, looking rather like an undersized collie, slunk along the floor of her kennel until she was within touching distance of Faye's outstretched hand. She turned her head to Rachel and showed the most amazing eyes, one brown and one bright blue.

'She's beautiful,' she gasped.

'Do you think so? Not everyone likes her. Very unusual looking, isn't she? Her owner died a couple of months ago and it seems she was passed from one member of the family to another, but nobody really wanted her. By the time she ended up here she'd become very confused.' She fondled the dog's shaggy head. Sally's mouth fell open and her tongue lolled out, making her look extremely silly.

'Can we let her out?' asked Rachel. 'She's gorgeous. I'd love to give her a cuddle.'

'Of course.' Faye unlatched the mesh door and gently encouraged the collie out. She watched Rachel and Sally greet each other with cautious interest. She nodded approvingly. 'She'll make a great companion for someone who knows how to deal with slightly, er, neurotic dogs. It's not everyone's cup of tea and she might be quite difficult to rehome. I don't suppose you'd like to foster her for a few days and see how the two of you get on?'

'Take her home?' said Rachel. 'Me?' Then she met the dog's mismatched eyes, and was lost.

It was much later than she had planned when Rachel left the kennels. There was a lot of paperwork to see to, but as each step was taken her excitement grew. She had wanted a dog of her own for so long, and now it was really happening. She hugged Sally to her, but not too hard, the dog didn't like that. Of course, officially this was just a temporary foster placement, but Rachel knew she would never let this sweetheart go. She needed someone to love, and so did Sally.

On her way home Rachel's thoughts turned, as they so often did, to Philip Milligan. He would no doubt think Sally no match for his beautiful pedigree dogs. Not that she was likely to see him. Why, she wondered, had he turned against her and the kennels? She couldn't understand it. He had tried to speak to her a few times since the party, but she had managed to find a reason not to take his calls. She was too hurt by what he had done, siding with Freddy Smith against them.

And then, as she rounded one of the last corners she glanced up to Freddy's farm. She didn't know what made her do it. You could glimpse a corner of the house and part of the yard from this point on the road, but she didn't normally have much interest in what was happening at Inshie Heights. Today what she saw caused her to brake, hard. That was Philip's four-by-four parked in the farmyard!

What on earth was he doing here? Without pausing to think, Rachel swung her own small car off the road and up the farm track. It was about time she found out what was going on. If Philip and Freddy were plotting something she was sure it wouldn't be good news for Collington Boarding Kennels.

The dog in the back gave a little whimper at the sudden change of direction and Rachel felt bad. 'Sorry about that, darling,' she whispered. 'Not far from home. We won't be here long, I can promise you that.'

When she drew up in the farm yard there was no-one in sight. She decided to leave Sally in the car, but wound down one window to give her some fresh air. She knocked loudly on the door, but there was no answer. Then she heard the sound of voices from beyond one of the barns and set off in that direction.

'At first she walked slowly, but there was something about the tone of the exchange that cause her to increase her pace. She was almost running when she rounded the corner to see Freddy Smith standing on a ridge that surrounded some kind of pit, pushing a stick down into the depths. What he doing? She hurried nearer. He couldn't be pushing Philip in, could he?'

'What's going on,' she said, covering the last few yards at a run. 'What on earth . . . ?'

The smell was almost overpowering and the sight equally horrifying. Philip was floundering in a pool of slurry. Freddy was reaching down with a long rake. 'Take hold of it man! Now! Take hold of it!'

Philip's expression was vacant and he made only a slight gesture towards the implement.

'Why doesn't he take it?' asked Rachel, dismayed.

'Get back!' shouted Freddy to her, taking in her presence for the first time.

Rachel didn't obey. 'What's happening? Can I help? Oh no, he's going under . . . '

Instead of moving towards the floundering man Freddy Smith jumped down off the ridge and began to pull Rachel farther away. He looked breathless and rather pink.

Rachel struggled to go back. 'We can't leave him . . . '

'Listen!' said Freddy, taking great gulps of air. 'This is really dangerous. Listen right now. It's the fumes that have overcome him and we risk them doing the same to us. I'm going to have to go in and pull him out, it's the only way. But I can't guarantee the fumes won't get me as well, if I'm not quick. I'm going to tie this rope round me and you're going to take the other end, do you hear?' As he spoke he was looping a rope around his waist. He made another loop which he kept in his hand and then passed the rest of it to Rachel. 'You hold on to this and help me out if you can. Under no circumstances are you to come over the ridge and you're absolutely not to go near the slurry, no matter what happens. Do you understand?'

'Yes.' Rachel understood all too well. She felt sick with panic. What if Philip had already gone under? What if Freddy couldn't get him out?

Despite Freddy's warning she had to go half-way up the ridge, so that she could see what was happening. She knew all about the dangers of slurry pits. Two local farm workers had been overcome by fumes and died not so very long ago. It had been all over the papers. What Freddy was doing, going down into the dark morass, was madness, but she didn't try for a moment to stop him.

Philip's expression was now completely glazed but he hadn't quite gone under. His head and one hand were still visible. Freddy slid down into the liquid with a loud gloop and made his way with difficulty towards the other man. Rachel held her breath as she got hold of one hand and pulled. Philip made no effort to help him. Freddy pulled harder and slowly the other man's body was drawn towards the edge.

Then, instead of pulling him straight out, Freddy looped the extra length of rope around his shoulders. 'Can't be sure I can hold him,' he called back to

Rachel, and already his voice sounded fainter.

His hands shook as he tightened the knot. Rachel wanted to scream at him to hurry, but she remembered what he had said about keeping back and dipped back from the ridge again to take a gulp of clean air.

'Now! Pull!' Shouted Freddy, and she did.

* * *

She never knew quite how, but with Freddy pulling the dead weight of Philip's body, and Rachel pulling him, they dragged the two of them out of the stinking pool, up the side of the pit and away.

Freddy collapsed for a moment when he realised they had made it, and then pushed himself upright again, he turned back to examine the other man. 'He's breathing, at least. Call an ambulance now, I'll . . . '

'No, you call an ambulance. I know

how to do resuscitation.' Rachel had already untied the rope to release Freddy and now turned to Philip. He was lying on his back, gazing blankly at the sky, his face an unnatural red.

He was breathing, but far too shallowly. She prayed that she was remembering this right and began the process of artificial respiration.

And gradually, gradually, Philip started to take in more air. His colour improved and his eyes seemed almost to focus.

'Rachel . . . ' he said softly, looking confused.

'You're going to be OK,' she said with a sob. 'Come on, let's move you farther away. Goodness, you gave me a fright.'

When Freddy returned to them they were sitting on the side of a stone trough. Rachel had splashed water over Philip's face and hands, and now she wasn't sure which of them looked or smelled the worst.

'He's OK,' she said to Freddy, although he could see that for himself.

'Thank goodness. The paramedics are coming anyway. They'll need to check him over. It was a pretty close thing.' He shuddered.

'How are you?'

'Fine. In need of a bath, that's all.' He sat down beside them and they remained slumped in silence for a few moments.

It was Freddy who first noticed the sound of a barking dog. 'What's that?'

For a moment Rachel couldn't think. 'Oh, that's Sally. She's my . . . new dog.' She eyed Freddy doubtfully. 'She's in the car, she'll be fine.'

After a moment Freddy rose and said purposefully, 'She sounds like she doesn't want to be alone. I'll go and bring her over.'

Rachel watched him in amazement.

'You've got a dog?' said Philip, frowning.

'Yes. A collie-cross, a rescue dog. She's not nearly as pretty as Bill and Ben, but I couldn't resist. I took one look and fell in love with her.'

'Looks like you'll have your hands full,' he said, watching Freddy lead the highly strung animal towards them. Sally was so delighted to be outside she was turning pirouettes and cartwheels, doing her utmost to tangle Freddy in her lead. Rachel waited for him to snap at her. He merely handed over the lead.

'Here, you hold on to her. I'll go and get us something to drink.'

Rachel wasn't sure what had happened, but something seemed to have changed Freddy Smith into a completely new man. She didn't have time to ponder that now. She concentrated on supporting Philip, who was still a little woozy, and thanking God that he was alive.

★ ★ ★

Philip was taken to hospital for a check up but quickly released. He was pronounced 'very lucky' and told to take things easy for a couple of days, but that there were unlikely to be any consequences in the long run.

Rachel wasn't so sure about that. One consequence was that she could hardly bear to let him out of her sight. She had gone home to clean herself up and then been taken to the hospital by her father. She was shaking so much he said it wasn't safe for her to drive. Maggie would have gone with them, if she hadn't been so busy making friends with Sally.

Philip's car was still at Inshie Heights Farm and he would need a lift back, but mostly Rachel just needed to see him. She felt an ache in her chest every time she thought of what the outcome might have been.

'How did it happen? Do you know?' her father asked as they neared the town.

'Not really. Freddy Smith says it was his fault. He seems really upset. Philip just said it was an accident and he was incredibly grateful to Freddy for rescuing him.'

'Freddy was very brave,' said her father, who had been told some of the events.

'He was, although he denies it. He says anyone would have done the same, but it's not true. He wasn't just brave, he was quick thinking.'

'And very lucky that you happened to turn up.'

Rachel gave a little shiver. 'Yes, very lucky. If he'd gone in there without a third person holding the other end of the rope . . . ' It didn't bear thinking of.

Philip's take on events was slightly different. Once they were back in the Collington's kitchen, with Maggie fussing around him, he seemed keen to laugh the whole thing off. 'What a fool I was. Should have watched my footing.'

'Freddy says it wasn't your fault. He's determined to take all the blame.'

'Least said soonest mended,' said Philip firmly. 'Thanks for collecting me from the hospital. And for fetching Bill and Ben for me. They must have thought I'd abandoned them.'

'They were happy to see me,' agreed Rachel. 'And they're charmed by Sally, the three of them are keeping each other occupied.'

'It's very kind of you, as I said, but I'm sure I could manage at home. You really didn't need . . . '

'The doctor said you shouldn't be on your own for the first night,' said John calmly.

'So it was obvious you should come here,' said Maggie.

'Who else would have you?' said Rachel with a grin. 'You're still just a little bit fragrant . . . '

Philip met her eyes, as though trying to understand her true meaning. Eventually he said, 'If it's all right with you, then, perhaps, I'd better go and have another bath.'

'Excellent idea. And then supper in bed,' said Maggie firmly. She loved to have someone to look after.

⋆   ⋆   ⋆

The last thing Philip had expected when he got up that morning was to find himself in the Collingtons' spare room, with a tray of delicious food on his lap and Rachel standing shyly beside his bed.

'I hope it's OK. It's Mum's special broth.'

'It smells lovely. Look, why don't you sit down? Will your parents mind if you stay and talk to me?'

Rachel hesitated. 'No, they won't mind.' She seemed nervous of him. Perhaps she was remembering, after all the excitement of the day, that the two of them hadn't been on good terms recently. Eventually she pulled up a little wicker-work chair and sat down gingerly on the edge of it.

Philip took a mouthful of the soup to fortify him, and then began, 'I suppose you're wondering what I was doing at Freddy Smith's?'

'Well, it's nothing to do with me . . .'

'What was it that brought you up there just at the right time?'

Rachel blushed. 'It was seeing your car, actually. I was furious, I wondered what on earth was going on . . . But as I said, it's nothing to do with me.'

'It has everything to do with you. I went to see Freddy to try and find out what is behind this vendetta he has against you.'

'So he really has had a vendetta?'

'Yes, I think so. Of course, I didn't help by making thoughtless comments about the flooding here. You do realise that was totally accidental, don't you? I never thought for a moment that it would come back on you like it did.'

'Didn't you?' Rachel realised how easy it was to say something without thinking about its impact. She did that all the time. Why should Philip be any different?

'No, I didn't, and I'm really sorry for the heartache it caused you and your parents.'

'I suppose a little comment wouldn't have mattered, if things hadn't already been so difficult, with the rumours Freddy had spread.'

'That's right. And I don't think he'll be spreading any more.'

'You've told him not to?'

'I was trying to persuade him not to. But I think the shock of my fall is what really changed his mind. He said he's been a fool to hold on to his own fears and that doing so very nearly caused another death. Did you know his wife died as a result of a dog bite?'

'Gosh, no. How awful.'

'Yes, it was. But I think he realises now it doesn't mean every dog is the devil incarnate, and nor are the people who deal with them.'

'So that's what it was all about.' Rachel shook her head slowly. 'I'm glad we understand. He does seem keen to be friendly now, doesn't he?' Rachel smiled, thinking how lovely it would be to have a neighbour who wasn't hostile to their enterprise. 'I hope it makes him happier, too. He has always seemed to be really bitter, now we know why.'

'Yes. I hope things work out for him.' Philip finished the last of his soup and put the tray to one side. 'Now, let's talk about something different. Like us.'

Rachel immediately felt very self-conscious. She had relaxed back into the little chair but now she sat upright.

'I think I owe you an apology,' she said quickly.

He put out a hand and took one of hers. 'No more than I owe you. But that can wait.' He looked at her so long and hard that she blushed. 'If all these misunderstandings hadn't arisen, would you have considered going out with me? Would you consider going out with me now? Or am I totally wrong when I think you might like me a little?'

He sounded so doubtful that all Rachel's fears fell away.

'Of course I like you,' she said softly. 'I like you a lot.'

'Thank goodness. Because I like you more than a lot,' he said, and drew her close for a long kiss.

* * *

Maggie glanced out of the window at the figure of John checking the dogs were safely inside their kennels. It was Bonfire Night. They weren't too close to town here, but sometimes the fireworks sounded very loud. As long as the dogs didn't have access to the outdoors, they were usually all right. He brought a couple of the more nervous ones to join Sally in the house.

'Just the two of us for tea tonight?' he asked as he washed his hands.

'That's right. And if I'm not mistaken it's going to be like that more and more, soon.' She smiled. 'Of course, I miss the children, but it's good to see them both so happy.'

'I miss them too, but I do like to have a bit of time on our own.'

Maggie nodded. They were very lucky. Even after over thirty years of marriage, they never lacked for things to say to each other.

She brought their food to the table. It was a new recipe she was trying, a mushroom risotto, and she did hope John would like it. He tended to prefer dishes that included meat but she was worried about his cholesterol and was trying to introduce some lighter meals into their routine.

'I wish Anthony would hurry up and make a decision,' she said as she took her own seat.

John smiled. 'Anthony's not very good at making decisions. Especially not in a hurry.'

'Perhaps I should set Rachel on him? She seems quite good at pushing him in the right direction.'

'Leave him be. If he wants to take up this printmakers apprenticeship Mr Randall has found for him he needs to be sure it's what he wants to do. It's a long training and the money at the end isn't good.'

'I wonder if we should have let him study Art at school.'

'He's finding his own way to where he wants to be. He'll be fine.'

Maggie used to worry about Anthony more than she had allowed her husband to know. But now she accepted that he was right. Anthony was finding his own way in life. Not one she would ever have expected, but he seemed happy enough.

The fact that the apprenticeship was in Glasgow, which would allow him to spend more time than ever with Gemma, was no doubt one of its attractions. She was pleased that he hadn't jumped at it immediately, despite this.

'Where are Rachel and Philip tonight? I presume she is with Philip?'

'Yes. With filming for his new series just starting they haven't seen as much of each other as they'd like. I think they're happy to have an evening together.'

'Do you think Rachel is enjoying her supply teaching? She doesn't seem as enthusiastic as I'd expected.'

Maggie smiled. She thought the lack of enthusiasm might be something to do with the fact that Philip had invited Rachel to go on some of the filming trips with him, which she couldn't do if she was working. 'And he's offered to pay everything for me, but I can't have that, can I?' Rachel had said to her mother.

Maggie had managed to say nothing. It wouldn't surprise her if Philip got his own way before long. He had mentioned to Maggie that he was hoping to take Rachel to a certain jewellers in Edinburgh at the weekend.

'And what about us?' John was saying. 'Now we've got the youngsters more or less off our hands, and your health has settled down, how about thinking about a little holiday?'

'Now that's a very good idea,' said Maggie.

It was just what John needed, he still tended to work too hard. 'I'll check our bookings and see if we can keep a fortnight clear. And maybe we should think again about downsizing a little. I'm not saying we should give up the kennels. I'm glad it didn't come to that. The bookings have picked up rather nicely since, well, since the rumours have stopped. But we don't want to get too busy, do we? Especially not if Rachel and Anthony aren't around to help.'

'Now the cashflow has improved, we can always employ someone if need be.' John nodded. 'Yes, I like the idea of providing work for someone from the community.'

Maggie smiled. She was never going to get John to stop thinking about others. It was one of the things she loved so much about him.

* * *

'Where are we going?' said Rachel.

Philip took her hand and smiled down at her. 'You'll see.'

And very soon she did.

He led her down one of the little vennels off Edinburgh's Royal Mile and brought her to a halt before a small window cleverly lit to make the jewellery displayed within glow.

'This is nice,' she said doubtfully, unsure whether this was their destination.

Now it was Philip's turn to hesitate. 'We don't have to go in if you don't want to. I just thought . . . '

Rachel turned to face him, her heart beginning to beat a little faster. 'Yes?' she said softly.

His handsome face was in the shadow of the tall buildings around them. Then he took a deep breath and pushed back the long hair she loved so much. She could see him more clearly now, and he looked terrified.

'I'm probably not doing this right. I thought . . . I wanted . . . ' And then he said in a rush, 'It would be better if we were together, wouldn't it? I miss you when I'm away and I think you miss me and I'm going to be away more than ever soon. So why don't we get married then you can come with me? I thought we could choose a ring but if you don't want to that's fine and . . . '

'Yes,' said Rachel firmly. She had never seen him so flustered. She stood on tiptoes and kissed him. 'Yes, I'd love to marry you.'

'Yes?' he said, bemused for a moment. And then, 'Thank goodness.' He held her tight. 'I love you, you know that, don't you?'

'Yes, I think so,' she said, putting a hand to his cheek. 'And I love you too. Even if you are grouchy and abrupt at times, not to mention high-handed, dragging me to the jewellery shop like this before you've even asked me . . . '

'Hey, I'm letting you choose the ring, aren't I?' he said with a grin. Rachel grinned in return. Why had she ever thought this man was dour?

'Come on, then, let's get on with it.' Then she added, ever practical, 'But you'd better tell me how much you want to spend, I don't want to bankrupt you.' 'It'll take a lot to bankrupt me. I'll have you know I'm rather well off. You won't need to work once we're married.'

Rachel paused in the doorway. 'And if I want to work?'

'Then you will, of course. I don't

316

mind, I really don't mind, as long as you marry me.'

Rachel didn't mind either.

★   ★   ★

Holding hands, they entered the shop. Rachel smiled around at the bright and sparkling baubles. But none of this mattered, really. What really counted was Philip's love for her and hers for him and their commitment to each other.

Her heart glowed warmer than any jewels. Now she had really come home, to Philip, where she wanted to be.

THE END

We do hope that you have enjoyed reading this large print book.

Did you know that all of our titles are available for purchase?

We publish a wide range of high quality large print books including:
Romances, Mysteries, Classics
General Fiction
Non Fiction and Westerns

Special interest titles available in large print are:
The Little Oxford Dictionary
Music Book, Song Book
Hymn Book, Service Book

Also available from us courtesy of Oxford University Press:
Young Readers' Dictionary
(large print edition)
Young Readers' Thesaurus
(large print edition)

For further information or a free brochure, please contact us at:
Ulverscroft Large Print Books Ltd.,
The Green, Bradgate Road, Anstey,
Leicester, LE7 7FU, England.
Tel: (00 44) **0116 236 4325**
Fax: (00 44) **0116 234 0205**

Other titles in the
Linford Romance Library:

ENCORE FOR A DREAM

Sheila Lewis

Limelight Theatre, struggling to survive, is temporarily saved when three sisters unexpectedly inherit it. Rosalind, Olivia and Beatrice are captivated by its charm and the loyalty of the company. With no theatrical experience, the girls strive to combine their own careers with working at Limelight — especially with Gil, the dedicated theatre director. However, an ongoing shortage of cash, a disastrous storm and unforseen tragedy threatens everyone's livelihood, while the girls also have to deal with personal emotional turmoil . . .

REAP THE WHIRLWIND

Wendy Kremer

Briana, passionate about environmental protection, is visiting Turtle Island in the Caribbean. When she discovers Phoebe, the elderly owner of the island, is considering selling it to Nick, Briana is concerned that he'd exploit the island. Determined to prevent this, she attempts to establish 'friendly tourism' there instead, although Nick is extremely sceptical. In reality he doesn't want to change a thing — but certainly relishes a fight. But when Phoebe has a heart attack, he blames Briana's new scheme . . .

IN DANGER OF LOVE

Sheila Holroyd

Ellie and the Earl of Arlbury were virtual strangers, but in a war-torn country they were forced to rely on each other to survive. Outside the normal rules of their society they developed a strong bond which drew them ever closer. But then it looked as if their luck had finally run out, the dangers that had pursued them from the start seemed to have triumphed, and they were threatened by a final, tragic parting . . .

LOVE IN THE MIST

Rosemary A. Smith

1883. Charlotte Trent has secured a post as companion to Lina, seventeen-year-old daughter of the handsome Richard Roseby, at Middlepark in Devon, and has promptly fallen in love with her employer. But not every-thing is quite as it seems at Middlepark . . . When Charlotte finds a bundle of old love letters hidden in her room she wonders who is Madeline? And the mysterious Anna? And what are Richard's true feelings towards the lovely, and recently widowed, Verity Hawksworth?